Victor Diniz, © SIMENON.TM

# GEORGES SIMENON

# *THE HAND*

*Translated by Linda Coverdale*

Georges Simenon (1903–1989) was born in Liège, Belgium. An intrepid traveler with a profound interest in people, Simenon strove on and off the page to understand—and not to judge—the human condition in all its shades. His books include the Inspector Maigret series and a richly varied body of wider work united by its evocative power, its economy of means, and its penetrating psychological insight. He is among the most widely read writers in the global canon.

Linda Coverdale is the award-winning translator of many French works and has been honored with the rank of Chevalier in the Ordre des Arts et des Lettres for her contribution to French literature.

## OTHER ROMANS DURS BY GEORGES SIMENON AVAILABLE FROM PICADOR

*Mr. Hire's Engagement*
*Tropic Moon*
*The People Opposite*
*The Man from London*
*The Pitards*
*The Man Who Watched the Trains Go By*
*The Survivors*
*The Krull House*
*The Strangers in the House*
*Strange Inheritance*
*The Widow Couderc*
*Young Cardinaud*
*The Mahé Circle*
*The Ostenders*
*The Snow Was Dirty*
*The Hatter's Ghosts*
*The Magician*
*In Case of Emergency*
*The Little Man from Archangel*
*The President*
*The Grandmother*
*Teddy Bear*
*Betty*
*The Train*
*The Others*
*The Patient*
*The Blue Room*
*The Venice Train*
*The Cat*

## *PRAISE FOR GEORGES SIMENON*

"A truly wonderful writer . . . Lucid, simple, absolutely in tune with the world he creates." —Muriel Spark

"He's a great writer of detail, of atmosphere. His descriptions of Paris influenced me." —Leïla Slimani

"He is unique and I do not mean just in our times, but in any times." —Henry Miller

"I love reading Simenon. He makes me think of Chekhov."
—William Faulkner

"An incredibly expert, dry, and inventive storyteller; the spell is infallible." —V. S. Pritchett

"I've read a lot of Simenon, who's a favorite writer of mine."
—Sigrid Nunez

"I want to know what goes on in people's minds. I suppose that's why I love Georges Simenon so much. He was such a master of the small domestic situation." —Ruth Rendell

"Elegant, simple prose . . . as pure as running water."
—Roger Ebert

"I really loved the Maigret books by Georges Simenon. He had a real sense of place." —Louise Penny

"Simenon is a master of the quick stroke, the spare narrative."
—Larry McMurtry

"Feels incredibly modern . . . A great writer." —Ian Rankin

"The greatest of all, the most genuine novelist we have had in literature."

—André Gide

"One of the most important writers of our century."

—Gabriel García Márquez

"Simenon has concentrated noir into a darkness as solid and heavy as the interior of a dwarf star."

—William T. Vollmann

"Simenon's genius . . . was for locating the criminal within every human being . . . Every one of his books is a dark mirror."

—Lucy Sante

"I would do anything for Simenon . . . We love each other with the skin of our souls, heart to heart . . . The novelist of complexes, malaises, mystery, of sticky and sinister souls, and the prince of friendship without shadow or stain."

—Jean Cocteau

"I am a fervent admirer of Simenon . . . He was a maestro."

—Henning Mankell

# *THE HAND*

# THE HAND

## GEORGES SIMENON

*Translated from the French by Linda Coverdale*

PICADOR
FARRAR, STRAUS AND GIROUX • NEW YORK

Picador
120 Broadway, New York 10271

EU Representative: Macmillan Publishers Ireland Ltd, 1st Floor, The Liffey Trust Centre,
117–126 Sheriff Street Upper, Dublin 1, D01 YC43


Printed in the United States of America
Originally published in French in 1968 by Presses de la Cité, France, as *La main*
This English translation first published in 2016 by Penguin Books, Great Britain
English translation published in the United States by Picador
First American edition, 2026

Illustration on page v by Maria Picassó i Piquer.

Cataloging-in-Publication Data has been applied for and
may be obtained from the Library of Congress.
Paperback ISBN: 978-1-250-42589-8



10 9 8 7 6 5 4 3 2 1

"Of course, they prefer that I not see certain things. But, above all, that I not tell them about others."

* * *

"Will you say everything?"
"Will you?"
"I will try. If I don't, I'll regret it the rest of my life."

—Georges Simenon, *Peuples qui ont faim*, 1934

# *Part One*

# 1.

I was sitting on the bench, in the barn. Not only was I aware of being there, in front of the sagging door that, with each swing, let in a gust of wind and snow, but I saw myself as clearly as in a mirror, noting the incongruity of my situation.

The bench was a garden bench, painted red. We had three of them, which we put away for the winter along with the lawnmower, the garden tools and the window screens.

The barn, also of wood painted red, had been a real barn a hundred years earlier, but was now nothing more than a vast shed.

If I begin with that particular moment, it's because it was a kind of awakening. I had not slept. Yet I was emerging, abruptly, into reality. Or was it a new reality that was beginning?

But then, when does a man begin to . . . No! I will not let myself go down that slippery slope. I am a lawyer by profession and have the habit, some even say the mania, of precision.

And yet, I don't even know what time it might have been. Two o'clock? Three o'clock in the morning? At my feet, on the floor of beaten earth, the pink filament of the small flashlight was still shedding its last gleam without illuminating a thing any more. With cold, numb fingers, I was trying to strike a match to light my cigarette. I needed to smoke. It was like a sign of recovered reality.

The smell of tobacco felt reassuring to me, and I stayed there, leaning forward, elbows on my knees, staring at the huge banging door that might collapse at any moment under the onslaught of the storm.

I had been drunk. I probably still was, which has happened to me only twice in my life. I remembered everything, however, the way you remember a dream when laying scraps of it end to end.

After a trip to Canada, the Sanders had come to spend the weekend with us. Ray is one of my oldest friends. We studied law together at Yale and, later, after our marriages, we had kept up the connection.

So. That evening, Saturday 15 January, when the snow had already begun falling, I'd asked Ray:

'How do you feel about coming along with us for drinks at old Ashbridge's place?'

'Harold Ashbridge, from Boston?'

'Yes.'

'I thought he spent the winter down at his home in Florida . . .'

'Ten years ago, he bought some property about twenty miles from here to play the gentleman farmer. He's always there for Christmas and New Year's and only goes off to Florida around mid-January, after a big party.'

Ashbridge is one of the few men who impress me. As is Ray. There are others. Actually, they aren't as rare as all that. Not to mention the women. Mona, for example,

Ray's wife, whom I always see as an exotic little animal, although as far as exotic goes, she's barely one-quarter Italian by blood.

'He doesn't know me . . .'

'At Ashbridge's, you don't need to know anybody.'

Isabel was listening without saying a word. Isabel never intervenes in such moments. She is the docile wife par excellence. She does not protest. She simply watches you and passes judgement.

At that point, there had been nothing to criticize in my behaviour. We went every year to that party at the Ashbridges', which is like a professional obligation. Isabel did not point out that the snow was falling hard and that the drive up to North Hillsdale is a difficult one. In any case, the snowplough had certainly gone by.

'What car are we taking?'

'Mine,' I said.

And at the back of my mind – it's only now that I discover this – there was a tiny ulterior motive.

Ray works on Madison Avenue. He is a partner in one of the biggest ad agencies. I see him almost every time I go to New York and am familiar with his routine.

Without being a drinker, he does need two or three double martinis before each meal, like almost all those in his profession who live on their nerves.

'If he drinks a bit too much, at the party . . .'

It's funny – or tragic – to recall those little details a few hours later. For fear that Ray might overindulge, I was taking precautions, arranging to be the driver on the way home. Except that I was the one who had got drunk!

At first, there were at least fifty people, if not more. An immense buffet was set out in the front hall, but all the doors were open, with people coming and going, even in the upstairs bedrooms, and bottles and glasses were everywhere.

'May I introduce Mrs Ashbridge . . . Patricia, my friend Ray . . .'

Patricia is only thirty. She is Ashbridge's third wife. She's very beautiful. Not beautiful like . . . I wouldn't say like Isabel; my wife has never been truly beautiful. Besides, I always find it difficult to describe a woman and I automatically do so in relation to my wife.

Isabel is tall, with a graceful figure, regular features and a slightly condescending smile, as if those with whom she is speaking were at fault in some way.

Well, Patricia is the opposite. On the small side, like Mona. Even more of a brunette than she is, but with green eyes. And Patricia, she looks at you, fascinated, as if she desired nothing more than to learn your innermost thoughts or to confide her own to you.

Isabel never conjures up the image of a bedroom. Now, Patricia – she always makes me think of a bed.

They say . . . But I pay no attention to what people say. First of all, I don't trust hearsay. And then, I instinctively loathe indiscretion, so I hate backbiting all the more.

The Russels were there, the Dyers, the Collinses, the Greenes, the Hassbergers, the . . .

'Ted! Hello!'

'Dan! Hello!'

People talk, drink, come, go, nibble things that taste like fish, turkey or beef . . . I had, I remember, a serious conversation off in the morning room with Bill Hassberger, who was thinking of sending me to Chicago to settle a legal matter.

Those people are rich. For most of the year, don't ask me why, they live in our little corner of Connecticut, but they have business interests more or less throughout the country.

Compared to them, I'm a poor man. Dr Warren as well, with whom I chatted briefly. I was not drunk, far from it. I don't know exactly when it all began.

Or rather, as of a few seconds ago, I do know, because on my bench, where I'm having at least my fifth cigarette, I'm suddenly discovering in myself a curious lucidity.

I went upstairs, for no reason, like others before and after me. I pushed open a door and quickly shut it, with just time enough to see Ray and Patricia in what wasn't even a bedroom, but a bathroom, where they were making love, completely clothed.

I may be forty-five years old, but that image made such an impression that I can still see it in minute detail. Patricia saw me, I'm sure of that. I would even swear that the look in her eyes was not embarrassment, but a kind of amused defiance.

That's very important. That image has considerable importance for me.

Sitting on my bench, in the barn, I had only a presentiment of this, but later on I had plenty of time to think about it.

I'm not claiming that it's what drove me to drink, but it was about at that moment that I began draining all the glasses within reach. Isabel caught me, and I blushed, naturally.

'It's hot,' I murmured.

She did not advise me to be careful. She said nothing. She smiled, with her terrible smile that forgives or that . . .

That what? Later. I'm not there yet. There are so many other things to work out!

One summer, I decided to clean up the barn, intending to empty it, throw things away and neatly arrange what was worth keeping. After a few hours, overwhelmed, I sheepishly gave up.

That's a little like what happens with another inventory, the one I undertook in the very same barn that night. This time, however, I'll finish the job, no matter what it costs and what I discover.

Already there's the image of Ray and Patricia to be properly filed away. And shortly afterwards, the look in old Ashbridge's eyes. He's no drunk, either, but a man who sips his drinks, especially after five in the afternoon. He's a bit portly, and his big pale eyes are always moist.

'Well, Donald?'

The two of us weren't far from the buffet, with several noisy groups around us. We could hear various conversations overlapping at the same time.

Why did I have the impression that we found ourselves suddenly isolated, he and I? Confronting each other, that's a better way to put it. For it was barely five minutes after the scene in the bathroom.

He was looking at me calmly, but he was looking at me. I know exactly what I mean. Most of the time, especially in such encounters, you don't really look at the other person. You know the person is there. You talk. You listen. You reply. You let your gaze wander to a face, a shoulder . . .

He was looking at me, and the two words he'd just spoken took on the tenor of a question.

'Well, Donald?'

Well . . . what? Had he seen, too? Did he know that I had seen?

He was neither gloomy nor threatening. He was not smiling, either. Was he jealous?

Did he know that Patricia was in the habit of . . . I was the one who felt guilty as he continued.

'Your friend Sanders is a remarkable fellow . . .'

Some people left. We could see them, in the entryway, putting on their coats and rubber boots, which stood in a row all along a shelf. Each time the front door opened and closed it let in a gust of icy air.

Then there was the sound of the wind, monotonous at first, blustery in bursts later on, and the guests began to look questioningly at one another.

'It's still snowing?'

'Yes.'

'Well, then, we're going to get a blizzard.'

Why I kept drinking, which was so unlike me, I still don't understand. I went from one group to another; familiar faces began to seem different to me. I believe I even sneered and that Isabel saw me at it.

A kind of uneasiness began to set in. Certain guests lived rather far away, some in New York, others in Massachusetts, and had up to forty miles to cover to get home.

I was one of the last to go. I heard raised voices, exclamations whenever a group was leaving and a particularly violent blast entered the house.

'In an hour there'll be three feet of snow . . .'

I don't know who said that. Then Isabel took my arm in a relaxed way, like a good wife, quite naturally. I understood nevertheless that it was time for us to leave as well.

'Where is Mona?'

'She went to get her mink in Pat's bedroom.'

'And Ray?'

Ray was in front of me, the everyday Ray, the Ray I'd been used to for twenty-five years.

'Are we leaving?' he asked.

'I think so, yes.'

'It seems you can't see a thing in front of you.'

I did not shake Patricia's hand the way I had those other times. I admit that I made this somewhat obvious, that I took a perverse pleasure in doing so. Did old Ashbridge notice?

'Get in the car, kids . . .'

There were only three or four cars left out in the driveway. The already savage wind was blowing so much snow hard into our faces that we had to walk bent over.

The two women climbed into the rear seats. I took the wheel, without Isabel asking me if I were in a fit state to drive. I was neither depressed nor tired. On the contrary, I felt pleasantly elated, and the roaring of the storm made me feel like singing.

'And that's one down!'

'One what?'

'Party . . . There's still one left, next week at the Russels', after which things will be quiet until the spring.'

At times the windshield wipers jammed for a moment before starting up again. The snow streamed by in almost horizontal white stripes in front of the headlights, and I used the black line of the trees to guide me because the edges of the road were no longer visible.

Behind me I could hear, in the warmth of the car and their fur coats, the two women exchanging banal remarks.

'You weren't too bored, Mona?'

'Not at all. Patricia is charming . . . Actually, everyone was nice.'

'In three days, they'll be swimming in Florida.'

'Ray and I think we'll spend a few days in Miami next month . . .'

I had to lean forwards to see ahead of me and several times I got out of the car to scrape ice off the windshield. The third time, I felt as if I would be carried off by the blizzard.

We have them every winter, more or less powerful storms. We know the treacherous places, the snowdrift spots, the roads to avoid.

How did we get back to Brentwood? Through Copake or Great Barrington? I couldn't tell you.

'This one is a beaut, Ray ol' buddy . . .'

A beautiful snowstorm. A true blizzard. When I turned on the radio, that was in fact the word they were using.

Up by Albany, they were already talking about winds of more than sixty miles an hour, and hundreds of cars were snowed in on roads to the north.

Instead of worrying me, the news excited me, as if I were welcoming with relief a little something extraordinary into my life.

We were not talking much, Ray and I. He was staring straight ahead, frowning whenever the visibility dropped close to zero. Then, on purpose, I would drive faster.

I had no score to settle with him. He was my friend. He hadn't wronged me in any way by making love with Patricia Ashbridge. I wasn't in love with her. I wasn't in love with any woman. I was content with Isabel. What score would I have had to settle?

I had to spend a few minutes manoeuvring around a snowdrift and used one of the bags of sand we always keep in the car trunk in the winter. I had snow in my eyes, nose, ears, and some was getting in through the gaps in my clothing.

'Where are we?'

'Three more miles . . .'

It was harder and harder to make any progress. Even though we'd seen three ploughs, the snow piled up as soon as they had passed, and our windshield wipers were now useless. I kept having to leave the car to scrape the windshield.

'Are we still on the road?'

Isabel's voice was calm. She was asking the question, that's all.

'I assume so!' I replied gaily.

The truth was, I no longer knew. It was only in crossing the small stone bridge a mile from home that I regained my bearings. Except that, after the bridge, the snow had formed an actual wall in which the front of the car embedded itself.

'That's it, folks. Everyone out . . .'

'What do you mean?'

'Everyone out. The Chrysler is not a bulldozer. We'll have to keep going on foot . . .'

Ray looked at me, wondering if I was serious. Isabel had understood, since this had happened to us twice before.

'Are you taking the flashlight?'

I removed it from the glove compartment and switched it on. It had been some months, perhaps two years, since we last used it and, as we might have expected, it produced only a yellowish gleam.

'Let's go . . .'

Things were still cheerful, at that moment. I can still see the women arm in arm, huddled forward, pressing on through the snow up ahead. I followed with the flashlight, and Ray walked silently beside me. No one said anything, actually. It was already rather hard to breathe in the blizzard without wasting more breath.

Isabel fell, got gamely to her feet. Sometimes the two women vanished into the darkness. I would shout, my hand in front of my mouth to ward off the freezing air: 'Yoo-hoo! . . . Yoo-hoo! . . .'

And a vague 'Yoo-hoo!' would echo a reply.

The flashlight beam was weakening. All of a sudden, when we must have been only three or four hundred yards from our place, it died completely.

'Yoo-hoo!'

'Yoo-hoo!'

I had to be quite close to the women, because I heard the snow crunching. I could also hear, to my right, Ray's footsteps.

My head began to spin. The energy the alcohol had given me was ebbing away, and it was more and more difficult to advance. In my chest, right where my heart was, I thought, I felt a pain that worried me.

Hadn't men my age, even strong, healthy men, died like this of heart attacks in the cold and snow?

'Yoo-hoo!'

I felt dizzy. I laboured with each step. I couldn't see a thing any more. I could hear only that aggressive uproar of the blizzard and I was covered in snow.

I don't know how long that lasted. I was paying no more attention to the others. I was still holding on, stupidly, to the dead flashlight, and was stopping every two or three steps to catch my breath.

Finally, there was a wall, a door opening.

'Come in . . .'

A gust of warmth, in the darkness of the house.

'And Ray?'

I did not understand. I wondered why the women hadn't turned on the lights. I reached for the switch.

'There's no electricity . . . Where's Ray?'

'He was close by me . . .'

I called to him from the threshold.

'Ray! . . . Hey, Ray! . . .'

I seemed to hear a voice, but it's easy to hear voices in a blizzard.

'Ray . . .'

'Take the flashlight from the night table.'

We keep a smaller flashlight on our night table because the electricity sometimes goes off. I fumbled my way slowly through the rooms, bumping into furniture I did not recognize. Then a gleam appeared behind me, one of the red candles from the dining room.

It was strange to see Isabel emerge dimly from the darkness holding aloft one of the silver candelabras.

'You found it?'

'Yes.'

I had the flashlight in my hand, but it was hardly brighter than the one from the car had been.

'Don't we have any spare batteries?'

'Aren't there any in the drawer?'

'No . . .'

I wanted a drink to buck me up but didn't dare have one. The women said nothing to me. They did not urge me on. Even so, I felt that they were sending me out, armed with a half-dead flashlight, to search for Ray in the blizzard.

I will say everything, obviously, otherwise it would not have been worthwhile to begin. And, first of all: at no moment of the evening was I completely drunk.

If I try to define my state as accurately as possible, I'd say that I possessed a warped lucidity. Reality existed around me, and I was in contact with it. I was aware of my actions.

Taking pencil and paper, I could record almost exactly the words I spoke at the Ashbridge party, in the car afterwards and, later, at home.

Suffering from the cold on my bench, however, where I lit one cigarette after another, I was entering, I felt, a new lucidity, which made me uneasy and was beginning to frighten me.

I could sum it up in a word – in four words, rather, which I seemed to hear out loud: 'You have killed him . . .'

Perhaps not in the legal sense. But then again, isn't the refusal to help someone in danger considered a kind of crime?

When I had left the house, when the two women had sent me out to look for Ray, I had gone immediately to the right. More precisely, to fool them, in case they'd been watching me from the window and seen the glint from my flashlight, I'd first walked straight ahead for a few yards and then, safe in the darkness, I had veered right, knowing that I would find the barn about thirty yards along.

I was physically exhausted and think I can say that my morale was spent as well. This enormous storm, this world gone mad that had earlier elated me to the brink of nervous hilarity, now suddenly scared me.

Why had the women stayed in the house? Why hadn't they, too, come along to search? I thought back to Isabel, impassive, looking like a statue with her silver candelabra held a little higher than her shoulder. Mona, her features blurred in the shadowy light, had said nothing.

Neither of them had seemed to understand that a real tragedy was taking place and that by sending me outside they were putting me, too, in danger. My heart was beating too fast, in fits and starts. At every moment I kept losing my breath.

I was afraid, I've already said so. I called out one or two times more.

'Ray! . . .'

It would have been a miracle if he had heard me, just as it would have been if he had glimpsed the glow, way too weak, of the flashlight through the snow falling almost parallel to the ground. It wasn't falling, it was whipping, thrown forward in actual clumps that hit you in the face and smothered you.

I heard the barn door creak and rushed inside, where I collapsed on the bench.

A red bench. A garden bench. I did see the grotesque aspect of the situation: in the middle of the night, in the middle of a blizzard, a forty-five-year-old man, a lawyer and respectable citizen, sitting on a red bench lighting a first cigarette with a trembling hand as if this were going to warm him up.

'I killed him . . .'

Perhaps not yet. Doubtless he was still alive, but dying, in danger of death. He was not familiar, as I was, with the area around the house and if he veered to the right, if he was off by just a few yards, he would tumble down a small cliff into a freezing stream.

That was nothing to me. I did not have the courage to look for him, to run the slightest risk. On the contrary.

And here is where I've arrived, where I am indeed forced to end up. Here is where I was heading little by little, on that particular night, the night of 15–16 January, on my bench, in the barn: what was happening to Ray did not displease me.

Would I have been in the same frame of mind if I had not been drinking at the Ashbridges' party? This problem is difficult to resolve and, in the end, does not change much. Would I have felt the same perverse relief if I had not pushed open the bathroom door and surprised Ray making love with Patricia?

Now, that's different. I'm getting to the heart of my ruminations. For what I was indulging in on my bench were ruminations rather than coherent reflections.

I had the time. I was supposed to look for Ray. The longer I stayed outdoors, the more thanks I would receive.

What Ray was doing that evening in the bathroom, with a woman he had known for barely two hours, one as beautiful and desirable as Patricia, was something I'd dreamed of doing a hundred, a thousand times.

He had married Mona, who, like Patricia, makes men think of a bed.

Me, I married Isabel.

I might almost say, 'That's all there is.'

But it isn't. I had begun, God knows why, tearing off a corner from everyday truth, begun seeing myself in another kind of mirror, and now the whole of the old, more or less comfortable truth was falling to pieces.

This went back to Yale. This went back to before Yale, before I knew Ray. This went back, in the end, to my childhood. I would have liked . . . Where are words when you need them! . . . I would have liked to do everything, be everything, be daring in every way, to look people in the eye, to tell them . . .

To look at people the way old Ashbridge does, for example, before whom, earlier that evening, I had felt like a little boy.

He didn't bother to speak, to strike an attitude. He didn't try to communicate. I was in front of him. Was he perhaps looking straight through my head? I was of no importance.

He was seventy years old and had never been handsome. He drank his little drinks that gave his eyes that glazed look, and dozens of guests had invaded his house.

Did he worry about what they thought of him? He provided them with food, drink, armchairs, open bedrooms, as well as the bathroom where Patricia . . . Did he know that his wife was cheating on him? Did he suffer because of it? Did he, on the contrary, despise poor Ray, who had merely followed so many others and who, within five minutes, would no longer matter, who already no longer mattered, whom Patricia would perhaps, that very evening, replace with a successor in the same or some other room?

I didn't admire Ashbridge simply because he was rich and had interests in fifty different business ventures, from commercial shipping to television stations.

When he had moved into the area ten years earlier, I would have liked to have had him as a client, to have acquired just a tiny part of his affairs to look after.

'One of these days, I'll have to have a talk with you,' he'd told me.

The years had passed, and he had never had that talk. I did not resent him for that.

With Ray, it was different, because Ray and I were the same age, had almost the same background; we'd studied the same things, and at Yale I'd been more brilliant than he was and he'd become an important figure on Madison Avenue, whereas I was just a plucky little lawyer in Brentwood, Connecticut.

Ray was taller than I was, stronger than I was. At twenty, he could already look at people the way old Ashbridge did.

I've met other men of their kind. I have some for clients. My attitude towards them varies depending on the day and my mood. At times I'm convinced that it's admiration. At other moments I admit to a certain envy.

Well, I knew this now, I'd just discovered it on my bench: it was hatred.

They frightened me. They were too strong for me, or I was the one too weak for them.

I remember the evening when Ray introduced me to Mona, who was wearing a little black silk dress, underneath which you could sense her body, alive in its smallest recesses.

'Why not me?'

For me, Isabel. For him, Mona.

And, if I chose Isabel, isn't that precisely because I never dared to speak to a Mona, to a Patricia, to all the women whom I've desired to the point of clenching my fists in rage?

The wind was blowing so violently that I expected to see the roof fly off the barn. Its upper hinge broken, the door now sagged crookedly, which did not prevent it from striking muffled blows against the wall.

The snow whirling inside the barn almost reached my feet, and I kept thinking in a kind of delirium, a cold delirium, a lucid delirium.

'I killed you, Ray . . .'

And what if I went to tell them this, those two women nice and warm in the house, in the candlelight?

'I killed Ray . . .'

They would not believe me. I was not even the man to kill Ray, or to kill anyone.

I had just done so, however, and this flooded me with a sense of physical joy, as if I had just cheered myself up with a potent drink.

I stood up. After all, I was not supposed to spend hours outside. Besides, I was frozen stiff and was scared about my heart. I have always been afraid that my heart would suddenly stop beating.

I plunged out into the snow that was hitting my face, my chest, enveloping my legs. I had to make an effort to hoist out one foot, then the other.

'Ray!'

I had to make sure I did not make a mistake and stray from the path. The house was invisible. I had taken my bearings when I'd left the barn. All I had to do now was walk straight ahead.

And what if I found Ray in front of the living room fireplace with the two women? I imagined them, watching me enter like a ghost, smiling and saying, 'Why did you stay out so long?'

That frightened me so much that I managed to walk faster, so that I bumped into the wall of the house. I felt my way along to the door. No one had heard me arrive. I turned the knob and saw first the logs burning in the fireplace, then someone, in an armchair, wearing Isabel's light blue peignoir. It wasn't Isabel. It was Mona.

'Where is she?'

'Isabel? . . . She went to fix something to eat. But . . . Donald!'

It was almost a shout: 'Donald!'

She did not rise from her armchair. She did not look at me. She stared at the flames in the hearth. Her face reflected no feeling; she looked stunned.

In a low voice she added, 'You didn't find him?'

'No.'

'Watching the time go by . . .'

Yes, seeing the time pass, she had begun to understand.

'Still, he's a strong man,' I said, 'more vigorous than I am . . . Perhaps . . .'

'Perhaps what?'

How to lie? And how could Ray have oriented himself in that ocean of snow and ice?

Isabel arrived, candelabra in one hand, a plate of sandwiches in the other. She looked at me; her face became paler, her features more rigid.

'Eat, Mona.'

How long does it take to die, buried in snow? Another three or four hours, and day would begin to break.

'Did you try telephoning?' I asked.

'The lines are dead.'

She looked pointedly at a small transistor.

'We've been getting the news every fifteen minutes . . . It seems the storm stretches from the Canadian border to New York. Almost everywhere, out in the countryside, the phone and electricity are cut.'

In a dull voice she added:

'Ray should have held on to your arm, the way Mona and I were walking . . .'

'He was at my right, not far from me . . .'

Mona wasn't crying. She was holding a sandwich and finally took a bite.

'Have you anything to drink, Isabel?'

'Some beer? Spirits? I can't fix you anything hot, because the stove is electric.'

'Some whisky . . .'

'You ought to take a bath, too, Donald. Later, there won't be any more hot water.'

It's true, the oil burner shuts down. Everything is electric, even the clocks, except for the little one in our bedroom.

Now I understood why Mona was wearing Isabel's bathrobe. My wife had made her take a bath, to relax as well as warm her.

'Did you go as far as the car?'

'Yes.'

Again, I felt a rush of fear. What if, while zigzagging in the snow, Ray had wound up back at the car? The smartest thing would then have been to shelter inside it, muffling up there as best he could to wait for daylight.

Our house, Yellow Rock Farm, is not on the road. We have a private access road of more than half a mile. As for the neighbours, they're about a mile away.

'From what I know of Ray . . .' my wife began.

I waited for the rest with curiosity.

'. . . he'll have pulled through . . .'

Not me, but him. Because it's Ray. Because it's someone other than Donald Dodd.

'Aren't you going to have a bath? . . . Take the candle . . . We'd best not waste them, and light only one at a time. Here, we have the fireplace flames.'

The radiators were going to grow cold. They were cooling already. In a few hours, there would be no more heat except in the living room. We'd be forced to huddle there, all three of us, as close as possible to the hearth.

It was my turn to carry the candelabra to find my way to our bedroom. I began wanting a drink again. Retracing my steps, I found Isabel pouring Mona a whisky.

I took a glass from the cupboard, picked up the bottle in turn and understood my wife's look. Still no reproach. Not even a mute warning. It was different. It had been going on for years, doubtless for as long as we'd known each other. A sort of official record.

She noticed things, without commentary, as if without passing judgement – and even forbidding herself to do so. The facts were nevertheless all there, in columns, perfectly organized, one after the other.

There must have been thousands, tens of thousands of them. Seventeen years of life together, not counting a one-year engagement!

I served myself generously on purpose, pouring the double – if not the triple – of my usual amount.

'Cheers, Mona . . .'

A silly thing to say, but she didn't seem to hear. I drank greedily. The warmth spread through me, and only then did I realize how cold my body was.

The bathroom reminded me of the one at the Ashbridges' house, and a thought of humiliating vulgarity occurred to me.

'At least he will have had one last pleasure . . .'

Why was I so sure that Ray was dead? The hypothesis about the car was plausible. Perhaps Isabel was right. She had no idea that I hadn't gone that far. He might also have reached, although that was more difficult, one of the surrounding houses. Since the telephone was out of order, it was impossible for him to let us know.

'I killed him . . .'

Mona had the same impression as I did; I'd seen that in her attitude. Does she really love Ray? Are there people who go on loving one another after a certain number of years?

Ray and Mona have no children. Us, we've got two, two girls, who are at Adams, one of the best boarding schools in Connecticut, in Litchfield, run by Miss Jenkins.

Did they have light, in Litchfield?

Mildred is fifteen, Cecilia twelve, and every two weeks they come and spend the weekend at the house. Luckily this had not been one of their weekends.

The water was running in the bathtub. I put my hand under the faucet in time to notice that the water was now cold, and I had to settle for a third of the bathtub.

It was an odd feeling, that night, to be an honourable man, one of the two partners of the firm of Higgins and Dodd, married, the father of two girls, the owner of Yellow Rock Farm, one of the oldest and most pleasant houses in Brentwood, and to think about having just killed a man.

By omission, true! By having failed to look for him.

Who knows? If I had spent hours with my dying flashlight, wandering in the snow, it is possible, even probable, that I would not have found him.

In my mind, then? That was closer to it. I had not searched. As soon as I could not be seen from the house, I had veered off towards the barn to take shelter.

Would Mona be in despair? Did she know that Ray was having sex with other women whenever he got the chance?

Who knows if she wasn't like Patricia? Perhaps Ray and Mona weren't jealous and told each other about their adventures?

I promised myself to look into that. If anyone ought to profit from that, it was I . . .

I almost fell asleep in my bath and was careful not to slip getting out of the tub, because I did not feel too sure of my movements.

What would we do, all three of us? Going to bed wasn't likely. Do you go to bed when the husband of a guest . . .

No. We wouldn't go to bed. Besides, the rooms were growing chilly, and I was shivering in my bathrobe. I chose some grey flannel pants and a thick pullover I usually wore only to shovel snow along the driveway.

One of the two candles was finished, so I lit the second one and put on my slippers to head for the living room.

'Do you know if there's more wood in the cellar?'

We hardly ever used any. We only had a fire in the fireplace when we had friends over. To get to the cellar we raised a trapdoor and went down a ladder, which complicated the fetching of any logs.

'I think we still have some . . .'

I looked automatically at the bottle of Scotch. When I'd left the two women, the bottle had been half full. Now it was almost empty.

Isabel had followed my glance, evidently, and – again evidently – had understood.

With another look, she gave me the answer, gazing at Mona asleep in her armchair, her face crimson. Her peignoir, in falling slightly open, had uncovered a bare knee.

## 2.

When I half opened my eyes, I was lying on the couch in the living room, where someone had covered me with the red, blue and yellow plaid throw blanket. The sun was up, but its light shone only weakly through windowpanes thick with frozen snow.

What first struck me, and had perhaps awakened me, was the familiar odour of ordinary mornings: the smell of coffee. Memories of the previous evening and night returned. I wondered if the electricity was back on. Turning my head a little, I caught sight of Isabel on her knees at the hearth.

I had a really bad headache and was not pleased at having to tackle the reality of a new day. I would have liked to fall back asleep but, before I had time to close my eyes again, my wife asked:

'Did you get some rest?'

'I think so . . . Yes.'

I got up and realized that I had been drunker than I'd thought. My whole body hurt, and I felt dizzy.

'Coffee will be ready in a minute.'

It was my turn to ask.

'Did you sleep?'

'I dozed . . .'

Well, no. She had watched over the both of us, Mona and me. She had been magnificent, as always. It was in her nature to behave perfectly, whatever the circumstances.

I imagined her, sitting up straight in her armchair, looking from one to the other of us, sometimes rising quietly to stoke the fire.

Then, at the first glimmer of dawn, snuffing out the precious candle and going to the kitchen to look for the pot with the longest handle. While we were sleeping, she had thought of the coffee.

'Where is Mona?'

'She went to get dressed.'

In the guest room, at the end of the corridor, with windows that looked out over the pond. I remembered the two blue leather suitcases that Ray had carried in the previous day, before the evening at the Ashbridges' house.

'How is she?'

'It hasn't sunk in yet . . .'

I was listening to the storm, still as strong as when I had fallen asleep. Isabel poured me coffee in my usual cup; we each had our own cups, and mine was a little larger, because I drink lots of coffee.

'We'll have to bring up some wood.'

There were no more logs in the basket to the right of the fireplace, and those burning there would soon crumble to ash.

'I'll go.'

'You don't want me to help you?'

'No, no . . .'

I understood. She'd glanced at me two or three times and knew I had a hangover. She knew everything. Why bother trying to deceive her?

I finished my coffee, lit a cigarette, went into the little room next to the living room, the one we call the library because one wall is covered with books. Folding back the oval carpet, I uncovered the trapdoor; I lifted it and only then remembered that I would need a candle.

All this is confused, unreal.

'How many candles are left?'

'Five. Just now, I got Hartford on the radio.'

It's the nearest big city.

'Most of the countryside is in the same fix we are. They're working everywhere to repair the lines, but there are still places they can't get to.'

I imagined the men, outside in the blizzard, climbing the poles, and the tow trucks making their way through the ever-thicker snow.

I descended the ladder, holding my candle, and went towards the back of the cellar carved out of the bedrock, the yellow rock that had given its name to the former farm. I was tempted to sit down to be alone, so that I could think.

But think about what? It was over. There was nothing more to think.

Now I had to bring up some wood.

My memory of that morning is vaguely sinister, like certain Sundays of my childhood, when rain kept me inside and I didn't know what to do with myself. Then I would feel that people and things were not where they should be, that sounds were different, both those in the street and those inside. I felt at a loss, with a small knot of anguish in the deepest part of me.

That reminds me of a silly detail. My father would lie in bed longer than on other days, and sometimes I'd see him shave. He came and went, wearing an old bathrobe, and his smell was different, like the smell of my parents' bedroom, perhaps because it was tidied up only later in the day.

'Good morning, Donald . . . Did you manage to sleep a little?'

'Yes, thanks. And you?'

'Me, you know . . .'

She was wearing black slacks and a yellow sweater. Hair and make-up just so, she was smoking a cigarette with a weary air while stirring her spoon in her cup.

'What are we going to do?'

She was just making conversation, carelessly, watching the flames.

'I think, at a pinch, that I can fix you some fried eggs. There are eggs in the fridge . . .'

'I'm not hungry.'

'Neither am I. If there's any more coffee . . .'

Coffee, cigarettes: as far as I was concerned, that was all I wanted. I went to peek out the door, which I had to hold tightly against the blowing snow, and could barely recognize our surroundings.

The snow formed waves more than a yard high. It was still falling, as heavily as during the night, and you could hardly see the red mass of the barn.

'You think we could try?' Isabel asked me.

Try what? Going to look for Ray?

'I'll put on my boots and sheepskin jacket . . .'

'I'll go with you.'

'Me too.'

All this made no sense, and I knew it. I felt like telling them quietly: 'It's useless to look for Ray. I killed him.'

Because I remembered having killed him. I remembered everything that had happened on the bench, everything I had thought. Why was my wife constantly darting glances at me?

In her eyes, I'd done some drinking, of course. That's not a crime. A man has the right, twice in his life, to get drunk. I had picked the wrong evening, but I'd had no way of knowing that.

Besides, it was Ray's fault. If he hadn't dragged Patricia into the upstairs bathroom . . .

Tough luck! I was going to pretend again. I put on my boots. I put on my sheepskin jacket. Isabel did the same, telling Mona:

'No, no, you stay here. Someone has to keep the fire going.'

We walked side by side, basically pushing ourselves through the snow, which piled up in front of us as we tried to advance. The cold stiffened our faces. My head was spinning, and I was afraid every instant that I would collapse, worn out. I didn't want to be the first to give up.

'It's useless,' Isabel finally decided.

Before going inside, we scraped clear one of the windows so we would now have some view of the outdoors.

Mona had returned to her place by the fire and asked us no questions.

She was listening to the radio. Hartford was announcing that roofs had been torn off, that hundreds of drivers were trapped on the roads. They mentioned the places most affected, but Brentwood was not among them.

'We still have to eat . . .'

Making up her mind, Isabel went off to the kitchen, and we were left side by side, Mona and I. I wonder if that was really the first time that we'd found ourselves alone in a room. Anyway, I thought it was, and that gave me an uneasy pleasure.

How old was she? Thirty-five? Older? She had done some theatre, a while back, and a bit of television. Her father was a playwright. He wrote successful musical comedies and had had a rather tumultuous life until his death three or four years back.

What was mysterious about Mona? Nothing. She was a woman like any other. Before marrying Ray, she must have had some affairs.

'All this seems so unreal to me, Donald . . .'

I looked at her and found her touching. I would have liked to take her in my arms, hold her close, stroke her hair. Were those the actions of a Donald Dodd?

'It seems that way to me, too.'

'You risked your life, last night, leaving to look for him . . .'

I kept quiet. I wasn't ashamed. Deep down, I was enjoying this moment of intimacy.

'Ray was a great guy,' she murmured a little later.

She was speaking of him as if he were someone already far away, with, I thought, a sort of detachment.

After a fairly long silence, she added, 'We got along well, the two of us . . .'

Isabel returned with a pan and some eggs.

'This is the easiest thing to prepare. There's some ham in the fridge, for whoever wants some.'

As she had in the morning, she knelt down before the hearth, where she managed to settle the pan on an even keel.

What were people doing in the other houses? The same thing, probably. Except that not everyone had a fireplace, or wood. The Ashbridges would definitely be obliged to postpone their departure for Florida.

And the girls, off at Adams? Did they have anything to heat with, up there? I reassured myself: Litchfield was a rather important town, and there had been no mention of power outages in the towns.

'The most powerful blizzard in seventy-two years . . .'

After the news, the radio went back to singing, and I turned the dial.

We had to eat quite close to the fire because at a few yards away you could already feel the bitter cold.

Why Isabel? . . . For as long as we've known each other, as I've said, she has constantly looked at me in a certain way, but it seemed to me that on that morning there was something different.

I even had the feeling, at one point, that her look meant: 'I know.'

Without anger. Not like an accusation. Like a simple observation.

'I know you and I know.'

It's true that my hangover was not going away and that at least twice I almost went off to throw up my lunch. I was anxious to drink something to get me back on my feet. I didn't dare.

Why? Always questions. I've spent my life asking myself questions – not many, a few, some rather idiotic – without ever finding satisfactory answers.

I'm a man. Isabel had found it normal, the previous evening, to see about fifty men and women drink beyond all measure. Well, I had almost felt that I should sneak those glasses I was grabbing from the tables and draining on the fly.

Why?

She had been the first, when we arrived home, to pour a Scotch for Mona, even though she was a woman, while I had waited a long time before daring to get myself one.

What was preventing me, now, from opening the liquor cabinet, taking out a bottle and fetching a glass from the kitchen? I needed a drink. I was literally staggering. I had no desire to get drunk, wanted only to steady my nerves.

It took me more than half an hour and even then, I cheated.

'Wouldn't you like a Scotch, Mona?'

She looked at Isabel as if to ask permission, as if my offer didn't count.

'Perhaps it would do me some good?'

'How about you, Isabel?'

'No, thanks.'

Outside of the evenings we spend at parties or giving one at our house, I usually drink only a single whisky a day, after getting home from the office for dinner. Isabel often has one with me, quite a weak one, it's true.

She is not a puritan. She does not criticize either people who drink or those of our friends who lead more or less irregular lives.

So, why that fear, for God's sake? Because anyone might have thought that I was afraid of her. Afraid of what? Of a reproach? She had never reproached me for anything. What then? Afraid of a look? The way I was scared, as a child, of the look in my mother's eyes?

Isabel is not my mother. I am her husband, and we have had two children together. She never undertakes anything without asking my advice.

She is nothing like the pushy, dominating woman so many husbands complain about and when we are with other people, she always leaves the talking to me.

She is calm, quite simply. Serene. Wouldn't that word explain everything?

'Cheers, Mona . . .'

'Cheers, Donald . . . And to you, Isabel . . .'

Mona wasn't trying to put on a show of grief. Perhaps she was suffering, but it must not have been a wrenching sorrow. She had said, as if truly from her heart: 'Ray was a great guy.'

Was that not revealing? A fellow something like a pal, a good friend with whom one has travelled a while through life in as pleasant a way as possible.

That was also what was attracting me. For a long time, I had had a sense of that peaceful and indulgent understanding between them.

Ray had wanted Patricia Ashbridge and he had taken her, without worrying – I'm sure of that now – about whether his wife would learn of it or not.

'I think the wind is dying down . . .'

Our ears were so used to the noise of the storm that we noticed the slightest change. It was true: we were still a long way from silence, but the intensity of the sound had dropped, and, looking out of the window we'd tried to scrape clear, I thought the flakes were falling almost vertically, although just as thickly.

Emergency teams were working all over the area to clear the roads, and ambulances were trying to get through to reportedly dozens of dead and injured.

'I wonder what will happen . . .'

It was Mona talking, as if asking herself the question. The snow would not melt for several weeks. Once the roads were cleared, they would deal with our access road. Then crews would undoubtedly come to look for Ray's body.

And after that? Ray and Mona had a handsome apartment in one of the most pleasant and elegant neighbourhoods of Manhattan, in Sutton Place by the East River.

Would she return to live there alone? Would she try to get work again in the theatre, in television?

She had been right, a little earlier. It was all unreal, incomprehensible. And I, during my meditation on the bench in the barn, I had not thought for one instant about Mona's future.

I had killed Ray, so be it. I had taken revenge in a rather foul and cowardly way, without worrying about the consequences.

In reality, I had not killed anyone. It was useless to boast. I could have floundered around in the snow for the rest of the night with absolutely no chance of finding my friend.

I had killed in thought. In intention. Not even in intention, because that would have required a cold-bloodedness I had not possessed at that moment.

'Maybe we should bring mattresses in front of the fire and try to sleep?' suggested Isabel. 'Not you, Mona. Let Donald and me do it.'

We went to the guest bedroom for that mattress, and then upstairs to get the two girls' mattresses, which were narrow and light.

I wondered somewhat foolishly if we were going to place them side by side, thus making a kind of huge bed on which all three of us would sleep, and I'm sure Isabel guessed what I was thinking.

She left about the same space between the mattresses that usually separates twin beds, and then she went to get some blankets.

I could be mistaken. I probably am. During the short time in which we were again alone, Mona looked at me, then at the mattresses. Was she wondering which would be hers and which mine? Was there, I won't say a temptation, but some vague notion in the back of her mind?

After Isabel had returned and spread out the blankets, we hesitated for a second. And, this time, I am certain of what I am saying. Isabel did not just happen to choose the mattress on the right, leaving me the one in the middle, and saving the one on the left for Mona.

She was putting me, on purpose, between the two of them. This meant: 'You see! I have confidence . . .'

In me or in Mona?

True, it might also mean: 'I'm leaving you free. I have always left you free.'

Or even: 'You really wouldn't dare . . .'

It was just past noon, and we all three tried to get some sleep. The last thing I remember was Mona's hand, on the parquet floor, between our two mattresses. That morning, in my sleepy state, was taking on an extraordinary significance. For a long while, I wondered if I would dare reach out my hand to touch her as if by accident.

I was not in love. It was the gesture that counted, the audacity of the gesture. I felt that it would be a deliverance. But my mind must already have been fogging over because the image of the hand turned into that of a dog I recognized, the dog owned by one of our neighbours when I was twelve.

I must have been asleep.

The electricity came back on shortly after ten o'clock that evening, and it was a curious sight to see all the lamps in the house suddenly turn on by themselves while the candle kept burning, almost ridiculous with its reddish flame.

We looked at one another, relieved, as if it were the end of all our problems, all our sorrows.

I went down into the cellar to turn the heat back on; when I came upstairs again, Isabel was trying out the telephone.

'Is it working?'

'Not yet.'

Once more I imagined the men outside, climbing the telephone poles with those strange metal half-circles on their feet that enable them to clamber up like monkeys. I've often dreamed of climbing poles like that.

'Where are we sleeping?' asked Mona.

'The bedrooms will take a while to heat up. We'll have to wait at least two or three hours.'

We did not talk much, that Sunday, neither during the day nor in the evening. If I were to write out the string of words we said, it wouldn't make three pages.

No one tried to read. It was even more out of the question to play any kind of game. Luckily there were the flames dancing in the fireplace, and we spent most of our time gazing at them.

We went to bed fully dressed, in the same places as that afternoon, but I did not see Mona's hand on the floor. At one point, I heard movements around me. I saw Isabel, standing in front of the fireplace, folding a blanket.

I didn't need to ask her what was happening. She had read the question in my eyes.

'It's six o'clock. The bedrooms are warm. It would be better to finish the night in our beds.'

Mona was kneeling on her mattress, her face flushed, her eyes dazed with sleep.

I helped Isabel carry Mona's mattress off to the guest room, where the two women remade the bed. I went to undress in our bedroom, then put on pyjamas and was in bed when my wife arrived.

'She's taking it quite calmly,' she said.

Isabel was speaking calmly herself, as if mentioning something of little importance. Later, she touched my shoulder.

'The telephone, Donald.'

At first I thought that someone had called us, that the telephone had rung and I thought immediately of Ray. Isabel had simply wanted to indicate that the telephone was working. The old clock on the chest of drawers said 7.30.

I got up. I went to drink a glass of water in the bathroom and ran a comb through my hair while I was there. Then, sitting on the side of my bed, I called the police in Canaan.

Busy . . . Still busy . . . Ten times, twenty times, the busy signal . . . Finally, a tired voice . . .

'This is Donald Dodd, in Brentwood . . . Dodd, yes . . . The lawyer . . .'

'I know you, Mister Dodd . . .'

'To whom am I speaking?'

'Sergeant Tomasi . . . What's wrong at your place?'

'Lieutenant Olsen isn't there?'

'He spent the night here, like the rest of us . . . Would you like me to put him on the line?'

'Yes, please, Tomasi . . . Hello? . . . Lieutenant Olsen?'

'Olsen here, yes . . .'

'This is Dodd.'

'How are you?'

Isabel could not see my face, since my back was to her, but I was sure that she was looking at my neck, my shoulders, and that she was reading me as well as if she were facing me.

'I have to inform you about a missing person . . . Yesterday evening . . . No, it was the evening before that one . . .'

The notion of time had already gone awry.

'Saturday evening, we went with two friends from New York to a party at the Ashbridges' . . .'

'I know about it.'

Olsen was a tall, blond man with an impassive face, high colouring, a crew cut. I have never seen him with a speck of dust or a crease wrong on his uniform. I have never seen him tired, either, or impatient.

'On the way home, late that night, we were stopped by the snow a few hundred yards from my house. The flashlight was going out . . . There were four of us, the two women in front, my friend and I behind them, trying to reach the house . . .'

Silence at the other end of the phone, as if the line had been cut again. It was irritating, and I could still feel Isabel's eyes on me.

'Are you there?'

'I'm listening, Mr Dodd.'

'The two women arrived safely. I finally reached the house as well, and it was only then that I realized that my friend was no longer beside me.'

'Who is it?'

'Ray Sanders, of the firm of Miller, Miller and Sanders, the advertising agency on Madison Avenue . . .'

'You haven't found him?'

'I went out looking for him, basically without any light . . . I floundered around in the snow shouting his name . . .'

'With the blizzard, he would have had to be very close to you to hear you.'

'Yes . . . When I felt my strength going, I went back inside . . . Yesterday morning . . . Yes, on Sunday, yesterday, we tried to go outside, my wife and I, but the snow was too deep.'

'Have you phoned your closest neighbours?'

'Not yet . . . I assume that if he were with any of them, he would already have called me.'

'That's likely. Listen, I'll try to send a crew over to you . . . It isn't snowploughs we need, but bulldozers . . . Only one section of the road is more or less clear. Call me if there's anything new . . .'

In short, we had done what we could. I'd put myself in a good position with the authorities.

'They're coming?' asked my wife evenly.

'Only one section of the road is clear. He says that snowploughs are not what are needed, but bulldozers . . . He's going to try to send us a crew, he doesn't know when . . .'

She went to the kitchen to make coffee, while I took a shower and put on the same clothes as the day before, my grey flannel pants and my old brown sweater.

Isabel had made some bacon and eggs for the two of us, and, since Mona's place was still empty, she told me:

'She's sleeping.'

I think she was a little surprised, though, by Mona's reactions, or, rather, her lack of reactions. Would Isabel have behaved differently if I had been the one to get lost in the snow?

Incidentally, I suddenly understood the strange emptiness I'd been feeling ever since my wife had touched my shoulder to awaken me: the wind had stopped blowing. The universe had fallen silent, with a silence that seemed unnatural after the hours of horrific noise we had just experienced.

I turned on the television. I saw shredded roofs, cars entombed in snow, trees knocked down and a bus turned over, in the middle of the street, in Hartford. I also saw New York, where men were trying to clear the streets, and a few dark figures were getting bogged down in the sidewalk snowdrifts.

There had been no news from several ships at sea. One house blown away by the wind. Another leaning crookedly, held up by a mountain of snow.

Snow: we had more than three feet of it at our own door and could do nothing but wait.

I made three telephone calls: to Lancaster, the electrician, whose house is a half a mile as the crow flies from ours; to Glendale, the chartered accountant; and lastly to a fellow I don't like, named Cameron, who is involved somehow in real estate.

'It's Donald Dodd . . . Sorry to bother you . . . One of my friends wouldn't happen to have taken shelter with you, by any chance?'

None of the three had seen Ray. Only Cameron asked, 'What's he look like?' before replying.

'Tall, brown hair, about forty . . .'

'His name?'

'Ray Sanders . . . Have you seen him?'

'No . . . I haven't seen anyone.'

When I returned to the kitchen, Mona was eating there. Unlike Isabel, she had not washed her face or brushed her hair, which was falling over her eyes. She smelled of bed. Isabel never smelled of bed; as my mother used to say, she smells clean. Mona's sloppiness and slightly animal casualness unsettled me, as did the questioning, indifferent look she gave me before asking in an artificial tone:

'When will they come?'

'As soon as they can. They're already on the way, but will have to wait for the road to be cleared . . .'

Isabel looked back and forth between us, and I cannot say what she was thinking. Although she could divine the thoughts of others, it was impossible to divine her own.

And yet, she had the most open countenance imaginable. She inspired confidence in everyone. In the projects she worked on, she was the one to whom the boring or delicate tasks were entrusted, which she accepted with her everlasting smile.

'Isabel is always there when you need her . . .'

To advise, console, assist . . . Outside of a cleaning woman, who came three hours a day and one full day a week, she took care of the house and the cooking. She was also the one who looked after our daughters until they went off to Adams, the boarding school in Litchfield, since there was no good school for them in Brentwood.

There was perhaps a certain snobbery in that. Isabel had also gone to Adams, considered one of the most exclusive institutions in Connecticut. Isabel was not a snob, however. I have lived seventeen years with her. For seventeen years, we have slept in the same bedroom. I suppose we have made love several thousand times. Yet I still cannot form a precise image of her.

I know her features, the colour of her skin, the blonde highlights of her slightly reddish hair, her broad shoulders that are becoming somewhat heavy, her placid movements, her bearing.

She wears a lot of pale blue, but the colour she prefers is a light mauve.

I know her smile, never too wide, a slightly fixed smile that still brightens up her already naturally open face.

But what does she think about, for example, all day long? What does she think of me, her husband and the father of her daughters? What are her real feelings towards me?

What does she think, at that very moment, of Mona, who is finishing her eggs?

She can't love Mona, who is too different from her and who represents slovenliness, disorder and God knows what else.

Mona's past is not simple and straightforward like her own. Some of it is rather dubious: the Broadway nights, backstage at the theatres, the actors' and actresses' dressing rooms, and her father, who saw nothing wrong with entrusting his daughter to one mistress or another.

Mona had not shed tears. She was not crushed. Instead she seemed like someone who feels that time is beginning to drag.

Her husband was out in the snow somewhere, one or two hundred yards from the house, a house that was not her home, which she wasn't used to and where she must have felt like a prisoner.

Now that the blizzard was over, that the snow had stopped falling, that the lights were back on, that we could communicate by phone and see the world live again on the television screen, we still had to wait for a crew to arrive from Canaan to begin moving thousands of cubic yards of snow.

'I'm out of cigarettes,' Mona announced, pushing back her plate.

I went to get her a pack from the liquor cabinet. It suddenly struck me that we had eaten in the kitchen, whereas when we have friends visiting, we always have our meals, including breakfast, in the dining room.

Even on our own, Isabel and I eat our lunch and dinner in the dining room as well.

We'd carried the girls' mattresses upstairs to the bedrooms, and the dirty glasses had disappeared.

'I'll give you a hand . . .'

Mona was wearing her black slacks, her canary-yellow sweater. She was helping my wife do the dishes, and I didn't know what to do with myself. I was thinking too much. I was asking myself too many upsetting questions.

Those questions could not all have sprung from the time I'd spent on the bench in the barn. Seventeen years had not passed without me asking myself some of them.

How was it possible that, until now, they hadn't troubled me? I must have answered them, automatically, with the appropriate responses, the ones you learn starting in school. Father. Mother. Children. Love. Marriage. Fidelity. Goodness. Kindness. Devotion . . .

It's true that I had lived like that. Even as a citizen, I took my duties as seriously as Isabel did.

Is it possible that I never realized that I was lying to myself and that in my heart I never believed in those edifying images?

In our office, it's my associate, Higgins (whom I always call old Higgins, even though he's only sixty), who takes care of the buying and selling of property, the mortgages, the company incorporations and, in general, all the technical business.

He's a chubby, crafty fellow who in other times could have sold quack medicines at country fairs. He's sort of grubby and untidy, and I suspect him of exaggerating the vulgarity of his behaviour the better to fool those around him.

He doesn't believe in anything or anybody and often shocks me with his cynicism.

As for me, my domain is more personal, because I deal with wills, inheritances and divorces. I have taken care of hundreds of them, because our clientele extends rather far beyond Brentwood, and many rich people live in the area.

I am not talking about criminal cases. I don't think I've had to appear before a jury more than ten times. I ought to know men. Men and women. I thought I knew them and yet, in my private life, I was behaving and thinking the way they do in what are called edifying books.

Basically, I was still a Boy Scout.

It's on the bench that . . .

I don't know where the two women are; probably in the guest room, and I'm wandering around alone in the living room and library, brooding over thoughts I'm not proud of.

And I had considered myself someone with a precise mind! The sight of a man and woman making love in a bathroom had been enough . . .

Because that was really the starting point. Apparently, at least. There must have been other causes, earlier ones, which I would discover only later on. It was on the red bench, in the barn where the door was banging, that a truth occurred to me and changed everything.

'I hate him . . .'

I hate him and I let him die. I hate him and I kill him. I hate him because he is stronger than I am, because he has a wife more desirable than mine, because he lives a life like the one I would have liked to lead, because he goes through life without bothering about those he bumps aside as he goes by . . .

I am not a weakling. I am not a failure, either. My life? I am the one who chose it, as I chose Isabel.

For example, had I known Mona at the time, it would never have occurred to me to marry her. Or to join a Madison Avenue ad agency.

Such choices I made through neither cowardice nor laziness.

All that is becoming much more complicated. I'm reaching an area where I suspect I will make unpleasant discoveries.

Let's take Isabel. I met her at a dance, in Litchfield, as it happens, where she lived with her parents. Her father was Irving Whitaker, a surgeon who was often called to Boston and elsewhere for difficult cases. As for her mother, she was a Clayburn, of the *Mayflower* Clayburns.

It was neither her father's reputation nor her mother's family name that influenced me. It was not her beauty, either, or her physical attractiveness.

I wanted other girls much more than I wanted her.

Her calm, that kind of serenity she already possessed? Her gentleness? Her forbearance?

But why would I have been seeking forbearance when I was doing nothing wrong?

In short, I'd needed to have things all compatible and well organized around me.

Whereas I feel raging desire for a woman like Mona, who is the complete opposite!

'The important thing,' my father used to say, 'is to make the right choice to begin with . . .'

He was talking about choosing not only a wife but a profession, a way of life, a way of thinking.

I thought I had chosen. I have done my best. I have worn myself out doing my best.

And, little by little, I have wound up hoping to see approval in Isabel's eyes.

What I had chosen, in the end, was a witness, a benevolent witness, someone who, with a glance, would let me understand that I was keeping myself on the right path.

All that had just cracked apart in one night. What I was envying in Ray, as in an Ashbridge, was their having need of no one, of no one's approval.

Ashbridge did not care if people mocked him because three wives in a row had cheated on him. He picked them young, beautiful, sensual, and he knew in advance what to expect.

Did he really not care at all?

And did Ray love Mona? Was it all the same to him that before he knew her she had been in the arms of so many men?

Were they the strong men and I the weak one, because I had chosen to live in peace with myself?

Well, that peace, I had not found it. I had pretended. I had spent seventeen years of my life pretending.

I could hear a rumble still in the distance, and when I opened the door, it grew louder. I realized that the snow-removal machines were approaching and I even thought I faintly heard men's voices.

Would they find Ray today? That was unlikely. Mona would be spending at least one more night with us, and I was sorry that it would not be, as on the first night, on a mattress in the living room.

I could see her hand again on the floor, that hand I had so longed to touch, as if it had become a symbol.

I was trying to escape. But to escape what?

For just over twenty-four hours now I had known that in reality I was cruel, capable of taking pleasure in the death of a man I had always considered my best friend and capable, if necessary, of provoking that death.

'You're going to freeze us . . .'

I swiftly closed the door and saw that the two women had got dressed. Mona was in a red dress, my wife in a pale blue one. They looked as if they were trying to get back to everyday life.

All that was still only a sham.

# 3.

Towards four o'clock that afternoon, we noticed through the window that the machines were slowly attacking the snow, cutting a trench there with walls as crisp as cliffs. It was fascinating. We said nothing. We watched without thinking. I wasn't thinking, in any case. Ever since Saturday evening, I had been outside my ordinary life and as if outside of life itself.

What I remember best was the presence of a female in the house. You would have thought that I could smell her, like a dog, that I went looking for her as soon as she left my sight, that I prowled around her, awaiting an occasion to touch her.

I had an insane, irrational, animal desire to touch her. Did Mona realize this? She didn't talk about Ray; two or three times, if that. I wonder if she, too, was not looking for some sort of physical release.

And there was Isabel's gaze, following both of us, without anxiety, with only a touch of astonishment. She was so used to the man I had been for so many years that she had almost lost the need to look at me.

Now, she sensed the change. She could not help sensing it. And she could not understand it all immediately, either.

I can still see the immense snow-removal machine appearing a few yards from the house, coming at us as if it were going to plough right through the living room. The beast stopped in time. I opened the door.

'Come in and have a drink.'

There were three of them. Two others were in a machine behind them. All five of them came in, stiff in their sheepskin jackets, their huge boots, and one of them had a frozen moustache. Simply their presence chilled the room. Isabel had gone to fetch the glasses and some whisky. They looked around, surprised by the intimate calm of the house. Then they looked at Mona. Not Isabel, but Mona. Did they, too, fresh from their silent battle with the snow, sense the warmth of a female?

'Cheers . . . And thank you for coming to our rescue.'

'The lieutenant will be along . . . He's been told that the road is open.'

They were the kind of people who pop up only on rare occasions, like chimney sweeps, and who live God knows where the rest of the time. There was only one face I knew, but I couldn't remember where I'd seen it.

'Well, thank you, too. This warms us up . . .'

'A refill?'

'We wouldn't say no, but we've still work to do . . .'

The monsters lumbered out, surrounded by white powder, and soon, as night began to fall, we saw the pale headlights of a car at the far end of the trench.

Two men in uniform got out, Lieutenant Olsen and a policeman I did not know. I was the one who opened the door, while the two women remained seated in their armchairs.

'Good evening, lieutenant. I'm sorry to have caused you this trouble . . .'

'You've had no news of your friend?'

He went over to bow slightly to Isabel, whom he had met several times. I introduced him to Mona.

'The wife of my friend Ray Sanders.'

He accepted the chair brought forward for him. His companion, a very young man, sat down as well.

'If you don't mind, Mrs Sanders?'

He pulled a pen and notebook from his pocket.

'Ray Sanders, you say . . . What address?'

'We live in Sutton Place, in Manhattan.'

'What is your husband's profession?'

'He's the managing director of an advertising agency on Madison Avenue: Miller, Miller and Sanders.'

'Been there a long time?'

'At first he was the Millers' attorney and for the past three years he has been their associate partner . . .'

'Attorney . . .' repeated Olsen, as if to himself.

'Ray and I, we studied at Yale together,' I added. 'He was my oldest friend.'

There was no point to all this.

'You were just passing through?' he asked Mona.

I was the one who answered.

'Ray and his wife came to visit us on their way back from Canada. They were to have stayed here this weekend.'

'Do they come often?'

The question threw me off balance, because I couldn't see the point of it. Mona replied instead.

'Two or three times a year . . .'

He looked at her attentively, as if her appearance were important.

'When did you and your husband arrive?'

'Saturday, at around two in the afternoon.'

'On your way here, did you have any trouble with the snow?'

'A little. We drove slowly.'

'You told me, Mr Dodd, that you took your friends along to the Ashbridges'?'

'That's correct.'

'Do they know one another?'

'No. As you must know, when old Ashbridge gives a party, he doesn't mind if there are one or two extra faces . . .'

A slight smile appeared on the lips of the lieutenant, who seemed to know a great deal about the Ashbridge parties.

'Did your husband have a lot to drink?' he asked Mona.

'I wasn't with him the whole time . . . I think he was drinking hard, yes . . .'

I had the feeling that Olsen had already made inquiries, doubtless through a few phone calls.

'And you, Mr Dodd?'

'I was drinking, yes . . .'

Isabel was watching me, her hands crossed in her lap.

'More than usual?'

'Much more than usual, I confess . . .'

'Were you drunk?'

'Not completely, but I was beyond my usual state.'

Why did I feel compelled to add: 'That has only happened to me twice in my life.'

A need for sincerity? Defiance?

'Twice!' exclaimed Olsen. 'That's really not a lot.'

'No.'

'Did you have a reason to drink that much?'

'No . . . I began with two or three whiskies, to put me in the mood, then I began emptying all the glasses I could get my hands on . . . You know how it goes . . .'

Very much the lawyer, I was furnishing precise details.

'Was your friend Ray drinking with you?'

'We ran into each other a few times . . . We'd exchange a few words, happen to be in the same group, then be separated again. The Ashbridge house is big, and there were guests everywhere . . .'

'And you, Mrs Sanders?'

She looked at me as if for advice, then at Isabel.

'I was drinking, too . . .' she admitted.

'A lot?'

'I think so . . . I stayed with Isabel for a while . . .'

'And your husband?'

'I only saw him, at a distance, two or three times.'

'Whom was he with?'

'With different people whom I don't know . . . He had a somewhat long discussion with Mr Ashbridge, I remember, and the two of them went off into a corner to talk . . .'

'In short, your husband behaved as he usually did on such occasions?'

'Yes . . . Why?'

She looked at me again, amazed.

'I am obliged to ask you these questions because they are routine when someone goes missing.'

'But it's an accident . . .'

'I don't doubt that, madam. Your husband had no reason to kill himself, correct?'

'None.'

Her eyes grew wide.

'Or to disappear without a trace?'

'Why would he have wanted to disappear?'

'Do you have any children?'

'No.'

'Have you been married a long time?'

'Twelve years . . .'

'Your husband, at the Ashbridges', did he run into any old acquaintances?'

I was beginning to feel uneasy.

'Not that I know of.'

'A woman?'

'I saw him with several women . . . He's always quite popular . . .'

'No arguments? Nothing eventful that springs to mind?'

Mona blushed slightly, and I'm convinced that she knows what happened between Ray and Patricia. Did she, as I did, start to open the bathroom door? Did she see them leave that room?

'You were among the last to go?'

Now it was obvious that the lieutenant had made inquiries.

'After us, there were only half a dozen people . . .'

'Who was at the wheel?'

‘I was.’

‘I have to admit that, given the weather, you managed very well. Four hundred yards more and you would have made it home.’

‘After the little bridge, there are always drifts . . .’

‘I know.’

For a few minutes I had been hearing a new rumbling outside. Turning towards the windows, I caught sight of a bulldozer in the now complete darkness, working in the beam of a floodlight.

Olsen understood my unspoken question.

‘Just in case, I ordered the search to begin despite the darkness . . . You never know . . .’

Know what? If Ray was still alive?

‘Once out of the car, you walked in the dark . . .’

‘The flashlight was almost dead. I preferred to have the two women walking up ahead.’

‘That was prudent.’

Sitting still on her chair, Isabel looked from one to the other of us, following the answers on each person’s lips, almost as if she were knitting with her eyes. She was knitting the images that, one day, would perhaps form a perfectly organized whole.

‘We two were holding tightly to each other,’ she said.

‘Were the men far behind you?’

‘Quite close . . . The wind was so loud that we could hardly hear them when they called to us . . .’

‘You didn’t have any trouble finding the house?’

‘Frankly, I wasn’t exactly sure where I was . . . I believe I made it here on instinct.’

'When you turned around, could you see the light?'

'At the beginning, a little . . . It quickly faded, then vanished.'

'How long after you got home did your husband arrive?'

She looked at me as if questioningly. She wasn't uneasy, and she did not seem to find these questions rather bizarre, either, under the circumstances.

'Perhaps a minute? I tried to turn on the lights and found that the electricity was off. I asked Mona if she had any matches. I went towards the dining room to light a candle in one of the candelabras, and Donald came in . . .'

What notes could the lieutenant be taking and what purpose could they serve for him? He was addressing me, now.

'Did you find the house easily?'

'I literally bumped into it when I still thought myself a certain distance away. I was wondering if I mightn't have got lost . . .'

'And your friend?'

'I assumed he was next to me . . . Meaning a few yards away . . . Now and then I would call: "Hey! Hey!" . . .'

'He would answer?'

'Several times, I thought I heard him, but the storm was so loud . . .'

'Then?'

'When I saw that Ray wasn't coming . . .'

'How long did you wait?'

'About five minutes?'

'Did you have another flashlight in the house?'

'In our bedroom, yes. Since we hardly ever use it, we don't check the batteries, and they were dead.'

'Did you go out alone?'

'My wife and Mona were exhausted.'

'And you?'

'I was too.'

'How did you find your way?'

'As best I could. My idea was to go around, making bigger and bigger circles . . .'

'You weren't afraid of slipping down to the bottom of the cliff?'

'I felt I could avoid it. When you live someplace for fifteen years . . . Several times, I fell to my knees.'

'Did you get as far as your car?'

I looked at the two women. I no longer remembered what I had told them about that. I had a sort of blank. I took a big chance.

'I reached it by accident.'

'It was empty, of course . . .'

'Yes. I rested there for a moment, out of the wind.'

'And the barn? Did you check to see that he wasn't in the barn?'

For the first time since this unexpected interrogation had begun, I was afraid. It was as if Olsen knew something, something I myself did not know, as if he were setting traps for me, looking innocent and scribbling in his notebook.

'I found it because the door was banging . . . I called Ray's name and heard nothing.'

'You went inside?'

'I must have taken two or three steps . . .'

'I see . . .'

He finally closed his notebook and stood up, like a soldier.

'My thanks to all three of you, and I'm sorry to have disturbed you. The work will continue through the night, weather permitting.'

And, to Mona:

'I suppose, madam, that you are staying here?'

'But . . . Of course . . .'

Where would she have gone, while they were searching for her husband's body in mountains of snow?

We had dinner. I remember that Isabel heated up some canned spaghetti with meatballs.

What day was it? Monday. I had done nothing all day but drag around. I had not gone to the office, which would have been impossible, but I felt guilty anyway.

In the morning, I am usually the one who goes to pick up the mail at the post office. My days followed a well-defined routine I had grown attached to. There was a time for each thing, almost for each action.

I still *felt* Mona's presence and wondered if it would happen. Not here, probably . . .

And why not? She had just lost her husband, whose body the dark forms and their machines were searching for outside.

'Ray was a great guy . . .'

Ever since Saturday night the three of us had been living on our nerves, Mona most of all. Isn't that the moment when you feel the need to throw yourself into someone's arms?

At war, men get rid of their fears through explosions of sexuality.

If we were to find ourselves alone in a room for long enough, safe in the knowledge that Isabel would not show up to disturb us . . .

Nothing happened. We went to the window to watch the bulldozer, and I barely found a way to brush against Mona's elbow.

We went to bed, Mona by herself, Isabel and I in our bedroom.

'What do you think of Olsen?'

The question startled me, because it showed which way my wife was thinking. And I happened to be thinking of Olsen as well.

'He's quite a good sort. People say he knows his job.'

I thought the conversation would continue, but Isabel left things there, without revealing whatever else was on her mind.

It was only later, when we were about to turn the lights off, that she murmured, 'I don't think Mona is suffering much . . .'

'There's no way to tell,' I replied evasively.

'They seemed much attached to each other . . .'

That word struck me. Attached! It's a common expression, I know, but I suppose people who use it have wound up forgetting its meaning. Human beings, two of them 'attached to each other'.

Why not 'chained'?

'Good night, Isabel.'

'Good night, Donald.'

She heaved a sigh, as on every evening, to mark the end of her day and the beginning of a night's rest. She was asleep almost immediately, whereas I would often try for more than an hour to drift off.

Mona was alone in the guest room. What was she thinking about? How was she lying in bed? I could hear the clanking sounds of the machines and I imagined the men somehow passing the snow through a gravel screen.

I woke up with a start in the middle of the night and, hearing nothing any more, I thought perhaps they'd found Ray. Why, in that case, had they not come to tell us?

I didn't move. I wonder if, in her sleep, perhaps sensing that I was awake, Isabel might have begun to listen as well. She did not stir, but her breathing became quieter. Everything was quiet, except an engine running, far away, over by the post office.

I was anxious, for no reason. This sudden peacefulness seemed like a threat to me, and I was relieved when I heard the machine abruptly start up again.

Had it broken down? Had they adjusted or greased it? Or had the men simply needed to take a swig of something?

I fell back asleep, and when I opened my eyes it was day. There was no aroma yet of bacon and eggs, but the smell of coffee already filled the house.

I got up. I put on my bathrobe, brushed my teeth, combed my hair and went down in my slippers to an empty kitchen. There was no one in the dining room either, or in the living room.

Assuming that Isabel was with Mona, I watched the machine at work; it had gone around the cliff and was now at the base of it.

A figure appeared at the side of the barn, and I was stunned to recognize my wife. She had put on my sheepskin jacket and her boots and was managing to make her way through the deep snow.

Did she catch sight of me in the window? The living room was in half-light, and I had not turned on the lamps. I don't know why I preferred not to be there when she came back inside. That visit to the barn had something secretive about it and was evidently linked to either the questions the lieutenant had asked me or my replies.

I retreated, went back to our room and ran my bath water.

I was hoping, without expecting much, that Isabel would come and join me, because I was eager to see if anything in her eyes had changed.

She had heard the water running. She had probably also heard Mona getting up, for when I walked into the kitchen, bacon and eggs for the three of us were on the stove, and the table was set in the dining room.

'Good morning, Mona.'

Today she was wearing a very clinging little black dress and, perhaps because her face looked tired, she was wearing more make-up than she had before, especially around the eyes, which gave her a different look.

'Good morning, Donald.'

I kissed my wife's cheek.

'Good morning, Isabel.'

She did not kiss me back. That was a tradition. I don't know when or how it started. It reminded me of my mother, who never kissed me and would automatically offer me her cheek or forehead.

I realized right away that Isabel had understood. I had also known, since Lieutenant Olsen's interrogation the previous day, what mistake I had made.

During the entire time I had been in the barn, on my red-painted bench, I had smoked cigarette after cigarette, lighting them one after another, simply dropping the butts to the dirt floor and rubbing them out with my boot toes. I'd smoked at least ten.

That's what Isabel had gone to get in the barn, while I was still asleep: the proof of my stay, of my sheltering there so long while I was supposed to be looking for Ray.

She knew. There was no hint of accusation in her blue eyes, however, no new harshness. Only astonishment, curiosity.

She did not look at me as a stranger because of what I had done, either, but I had become someone else, someone she had known for a long time without intuiting his true personality.

While we ate we could hear the men working at the base of the cliff. Mona, intrigued by the quality of our silence, looked from one to the other of us and wondered, perhaps, if my wife might be jealous.

This showed in a short remark: 'I'm ashamed to be imposing myself for so long . . .'

'Don't be silly, Mona. You know perfectly well that we think of you and Ray as family . . .'

I felt uncomfortable and ate quickly. As I stood up I announced, 'I'm going to see if I can go and get the car.'

I put on my boots, my jacket, my fur hat. I had the feeling that Mona was going to offer to go with me, for a change of air, but she did not dare to.

Below the cliff the men were working more carefully, having reached the place where they were most likely to find the body.

I followed the trench, where the frozen pathway had become slippery, and I felt liberated at being outdoors in the fresh air, once again recognizing my changed but still familiar surroundings.

The men had pushed my car, still covered with snow, up against the side of the trench. I had to clear the windshield. I wasn't sure if the engine would start. It seemed as if a long time had passed and that major difficulties must have ensued.

Well, the Chrysler purred immediately into action, and I drove it, carefully, to our garage. This was a small wooden building painted white, facing the barn. I had to clear some space with a shovel to open the garage door and inside I saw the Lincoln convertible Ray and Mona had driven down from Canada on Saturday afternoon.

A few minutes later, I entered the barn; the big door had collapsed outside the building. There was a large patch of snow, but it did not reach the area around the bench. I looked at the ground.

The cigarette butts were gone.

When I went back inside, I looked immediately into her eyes, and she did not turn away but looked back openly, calmly. What could I read there?

'So! . . . I know! . . . I had suspected it . . . When you answered Olsen about the barn, I understood . . . I went to see and arranged things so that others wouldn't know . . .'

Wouldn't know that I was a coward? Did she think it was because of physical cowardice, because I was afraid of getting lost in the blizzard, that I had taken refuge in the barn?

Why, then, was there no contempt in her eyes? No pity, either. No anger. Nothing.

Wait, yes! Curiosity.

'You didn't have any trouble with the car?' she asked, a little too brightly.

'No.'

'Aren't you going to the office?'

'I'll call Helen to have her get the mail . . . There shouldn't be any, because the delivery trucks have probably been unable to make their rounds . . .'

We were talking to no purpose. She had seen me go inside the barn. So I had to know that she had removed the cigarette butts.

The dishes were already done. We looked at one another, all three of us, not knowing where to go or what to do. Mona felt even more strongly that something was happening and announced uncertainly:

'I'm going to straighten up my room.'

The cleaning lady had not come. She lived beyond the hill, and the road that led through the woods to the village was probably not clear.

'Actually, I will go in, as far as the office.'

It was unbearable to be shut up like that, waiting for the men to find the body. I got out the car I had just put away moments before.

Once off the property, I found the road clearer, with signs that several cars had already passed that way. The main road looked almost normal, except for the height of the snow piled at either side.

Most of the shopkeepers were busy with shovels, cutting paths to their stores. The post office was open, and I went in, waving to the cashier as usual, as if nothing had happened. In our post office box I found only a few letters and a handful of brochures. Then I went to the office.

Here as well, nothing had changed. Higgins was in his room and looked up at me in some surprise.

'So, they finally found him?'

I frowned.

'Your friend Sanders . . . Are they still rummaging in the snow?'

Five years earlier, we had built an attractive building of pink brick and white stone window surrounds on the site of the old offices. The door was white. The well-kept surrounding lawn was not visible for the moment, of course, but every year the grass sprang up into the sunlight by the middle or end of March.

Helen, our secretary, was typing in her office and did not stop work to greet me.

Everything was calm, orderly; my law books were in place in the mahogany bookcases. The hands of the electric clock advanced silently. I sat down in my chair and opened the envelopes one by one.

'Helen . . .'

'Yes, Mr Dodd . . .'

She was twenty-five and rather pretty. She was the daughter of one of our clients, a building contractor, and she had got married six months earlier.

Would she stay with us if she had a child? She claimed that she would. I wasn't so sure of that and I anticipated having to find someone to replace her.

I dictated three unimportant letters.

'The others are for Higgins.'

Had Isabel been shocked? Was our life going to be disturbed because of this? I wondered, without knowing if I desired that or not. The exaltation of the night in the barn had died down, yet something still remained of it.

My wife was right to look at me curiously. I was no longer the same man. Higgins had not noticed this. Neither had my secretary. Sooner or later, they would discover the transformation.

I checked the time as if I had an appointment. And I did have one, in fact. Only, it had no appointed time. I was eager to have done with the search out at Yellow Rock Farm, eager to have Ray's body found. I was eager to be rid of it.

What would they do with it when they finally found it? That was not my business. That was Mona's concern. She was busy making her bed, tidying her room.

There were no newspapers. The New York train had not arrived. Much quicker than I had expected, Helen brought me my three letters to sign.

'I'm going home. If something comes up, just call me.'

I walked past Higgins' office and shook his hand.

Outside, I decided that it wouldn't be a bad idea to buy some meat and I went to the supermarket.

'Have they found your friend, Mr Dodd?'

'Not yet.'

'When you think that such things happen right next to us and we don't even notice! . . . Did you have any damage?'

'Only the barn door.'

'A house was blown away, in Cresthill . . . It's a miracle that no one was killed.'

Cresthill is where our cleaning lady lived.

Even though I was talking, looking around, going through the everyday motions, I was constantly asking myself: 'What does she think?'

From what I knew of her, she would not talk to me about it. Life would go on as always, with this secret between us. Now and then, I would feel her gaze on me, doubtless reflecting the same astonishment.

Turning left toward our drive, I noticed that the machines were no longer running and a few moments later I saw from a distance the two women leaving the house in boots and heavy jackets. At the base of the cliff, men were standing around a form lying on the ground.

They had found Ray. I put the car in the garage. I was calm. I felt no remorse. I experienced, on the contrary, immense relief.

The women waited for me before going down the slope. I gave each of them a hand, which didn't prevent us from slipping, and the machine operators had to help us up.

Ray seemed to be smiling under the fine sprinkling of snow that still covered his face and whitened his hair. His right leg was twisted, and one of the men told us it was broken.

I wondered what Mona would do. She did not throw herself on the body. Perhaps she had wanted to for a moment, because she took two or three steps forward; then she stopped, staring and shivering. My wife was on her right, I was to her left. It was to me she turned ever so slightly, just enough to touch my shoulder and side, as if she'd needed my warmth. Then, looking at Isabel, I put my arm around her shoulders.

'Be brave, Mona . . .'

It was a natural thing to do. She was the wife of my best friend. The men around us seemed completely unfazed. Far from being offended, Mona seemed to press even closer to me.

Only I felt it necessary to shoot Isabel a look of defiance.

It represented another step, as if, with this apparently simple gesture, I were assuring her of my emancipation.

She did not flinch and turned again to the body, which she contemplated with clasped hands, as one considers a coffin descending into the grave.

'Do you want to move him into the house?'

The crew chief stepped forward.

'The lieutenant advised us not to do anything until he arrived.'

'Did you telephone him?'

'Yes. I had instructions.'

We couldn't stay there in the cold, standing deep in the snow, waiting for the lieutenant to arrive from Canaan.

'Mona, come . . .'

I thought she was going to protest, but she allowed herself to be led away, and we had to climb the hill. I no longer had my arm around her shoulders, but I had done it. It was a victory.

'I suppose he slipped,' she said, once we were back up. 'Poor Ray . . .'

The three of us were walking, three dark figures in the white scenery, and I felt that this must be grotesque. Below, the men started up their machine again to disengage it and probably go and work somewhere else.

'Would you make some coffee, Isabel?'

We followed her into the kitchen, where she set water to boil. She was the one who asked the question.

'What are you going to do, Mona?'

'I don't know.'

'Does he still have any family?'

'A brother who's an embassy attaché in Germany . . .'

'Didn't he ever tell you anything?'

'About what?'

'The arrangements to make in the event . . .'

Calmly, she searched for the words and found them.

'. . . in the event of an accident.'

'He never talked about that.'

'The thing is, there are arrangements to be made,' continued Isabel, thus taking on the most unpleasant tasks. 'Do you think he left a will?'

Mona and I said no at the same time.

'If Ray had drawn up a will,' I explained, 'he would have done it with me and left it with me as well.'

'Do you think, Mona, that he would have preferred cremation?'

'I don't know . . .'

We each took our cup of coffee into the living room; out the window we could see the police car arrive and the lieutenant and another officer go down to the base of the cliff.

Within ten minutes, the lieutenant appeared alone at the door and removed his cap.

'May I offer you my condolences, Mrs Sanders . . .'

'Thank you.'

'It's just what you thought, Mr Dodd. He swerved over towards the cliff and slipped, fracturing a leg in his fall . . .'

Had I said that to him? I no longer remembered. I think he, too, was looking at me in a different way.

'I'll have the body taken to the funeral home, and you will merely have to give them their instructions.'

'Yes,' murmured Mona, who did not seem to understand what was expected of her.

'Where do you intend to have him buried?'

'I don't know . . .'

'At Pleasantville,' I suggested.

It was the large cemetery in New York.

'Probably . . .'

'Is there any family?'

'A brother, in Germany . . .'

We began again. Words. Lips moving. But I was not listening to the words. I was watching the eyes. I think that I have always watched the eyes. Or, rather, that I have always been a little afraid of them.

There were Isabel's eyes. Those I was familiar with. I had known since that morning what astonishment they expressed.

Yet she was the one carefully watching the lieutenant. She had realized that he was glancing at me from time to time, as if something about this business were bothering him.

I am convinced that if the lieutenant had attacked me, she would have come to my rescue. You'd have thought she was waiting only for that moment.

As for Mona, it was towards me that she turned whenever she was asked a question, as if I had naturally become her chief support. This was so apparent, and her attitude revealed such confidence and surrender, that Olsen must have thought we were bound by some intimate relationship.

Was that why he was less cordial towards me? A trifle contemptuous, I thought.

'I will leave you to do what is needed. As far as we're concerned, the case is closed. I regret, Mrs Sanders, that this tragedy took place here in our town.'

He rose, bowed to the two women and finally held out his hand to me. In good faith? I'm not so sure.

I suspect that he's hiding something. Either his men found something suspicious that puts me in a tricky position, or else Olsen, believing me to be the lover of my best friend's wife, despises me.

Would he suspect me of taking advantage of the chance to push Ray off the cliff?

I hadn't thought of that before. It was so plausible, so easy! And why, first of all, did I have the two women walking ahead, when I carried the only – albeit feeble – flashlight we possessed?

I was the one most familiar with the cliff, since it's on my property, in front of my windows. I could hold Ray by the arm, lead him off to the right, push him at the proper moment . . .

I was scared to think that Olsen might have found the cigarette butts in front of the bench in the barn. Would he have come to the same conclusions as Isabel?

Exactly what were Isabel's conclusions? What proved to me that she did not, in fact, believe that I had pushed Ray?

In which case, her silence became a kind of complicity . . . The defence of her home, our two children . . .

She kept her eyes on me when I opened the liquor cabinet.

'A drink will do you good, Mona. Would you like one too, Isabel?'

'No, thanks.'

I went to get the glasses and ice from the kitchen. Holding her drink out to Mona, I said:

'Courage, my dear Mona . . .'

As if I were staking my claim. This time, Isabel noticed and for a moment seemed startled. I had never called her that: my dear Mona . . .

'I'm going to telephone the funeral parlour,' announced Isabel, heading for the library to use one of our two telephones.

Was it to leave us alone?

After taking a swallow, Mona turned to me, smiling a little sadly.

'You're a nice man, Donald.'

Then, after a glance where Isabel had just gone, she seemed about to add something, but in the end said nothing.

# 4.

The funeral took place Thursday morning and did not proceed as I had envisioned when the three of us were still off alone in our house.

There must be some catastrophes that are like illnesses. You think that it will take a long time to get well, that life will no longer be the same, and then you see that daily routine takes over again.

At ten o'clock, there were more than twenty cars in front of the Fred Dowling Funeral Home, barely a hundred yards from my office, and two of them had brought reporters and photographers from New York.

Some of them had come to the house the previous day. They had insisted that Mona pose at the spot where Ray's body had been found.

Bob Sanders had arrived the day before from Bonn. Isabel had offered him one of the girls' bedrooms for the night, but he had already reserved a room at the Turley Hotel.

He was taller, thinner, more nonchalant than Ray. He was even more casual in his behaviour than his brother was, and I did not like the self-satisfaction of his smile.

I had met him a few times when we were students, but he was much younger than Ray and I were, and I had barely paid attention to him.

He did not show much consideration to Mona.

'How did it happen? He'd been drinking?'

'Not more than usual . . .'

'Had he started to drink a lot?'

Ray was five years older than he was, and he spoke of him rather like a judge preparing to deliver a verdict.

'No . . . Two or three martinis before meals . . .'

The brother was born near New Haven and he knew about our climate. He must have experienced blizzards, not as fierce as the one last Saturday, but still just as disruptive.

'How come they didn't find him sooner?'

'In some places the snow was more than six feet deep . . .'

'What arrangements have you made?'

He didn't like me, either. He frowned at me now and then, perhaps finding that I had been very quick to take Mona under my protection.

Because I was doing that, openly, on purpose. I kept close to her. I was the one who answered most of the questions and I could tell that it exasperated Bob Sanders.

'Whom have you told about this?'

'His associates, of course . . .'

'Were you the one who informed the newspapers?'

'No. That must have been someone in the village, maybe one of the policemen . . . A Scotch?'

'No, thanks. I don't drink.'

He had rented himself a car at the airport. He was married. His wife and three children lived in Bonn with him. He had come over alone. I'm fairly sure he had not seen Ray for several years.

As for the Miller brothers, they did not bother stopping by the house. It was only at the funeral parlour that they went over to Mona to offer their condolences.

I knew one of them, Samuel, having lunched with him and Ray once in New York: a man of about sixty, bald and jovial.

He approached me to ask quietly, 'Do you know who's handling the estate?'

'That is Mona's business.'

'She hasn't talked to you about it?'

'Not yet . . .'

He went to speak to the brother as well, whom he must have asked the same question, because Bob Sanders shook his head.

Mona was driving her own car, since she would be going directly on from Pleasantville to New York. Although I had suggested that Isabel drive, Mona had said no to that, but had welcomed her company.

Behind the two women came the brother's car, then mine, then the chauffeured limousine belonging to the Miller brothers, who looked like twins. Other Madison Avenue people followed, including Ray's secretary, a tall, statuesque redhead who seemed more grief-stricken than Mona.

Many people whom I did not know. No announcements had been sent out, but the time and place of the funeral had been published in the papers.

I was familiar with the road, which was still bordered by mounds of snow, and the sun came out after only a few miles.

Mona had confided something strange to me the previous day; we had been alone in the living room while Isabel was out running some errands.

'You're the only one I can tell this to, Donald . . . I'm wondering if Ray didn't do it on purpose . . .'

Nothing she could have said would have surprised me more.

'You mean that he might have committed suicide?'

'I don't like that word. He might have helped fate along . . .'

'He had problems?'

'Not in business . . . In that department, he was succeeding beyond his hopes . . .'

'In his private life?'

'Not there, either . . . We were great pals, the two of us . . . He told me everything . . . Or almost everything. We didn't show off or play-act in front of each other . . .'

I was struck by those words. So, there were some people who could behave naturally, face to face? Was that what Isabel had been seeking in my eyes for so many years? That I reveal myself? That I confess to her for once what was weighing on my mind?

'Affairs . . . He had a lot of them. Starting with his secretary, that tall redhead, Hilda.'

She was the woman who had followed in one of the cars.

'It's hard to explain, Donald . . . I wonder if he didn't envy you . . .'

'Me?'

'You studied the same things . . . He could have become a lawyer, that was his ambition when he started out in

New York. Then he became legal counsel in that ad agency . . . He began to earn money and realized that he'd make more by selling contracts.

'You see what I mean? He became a businessman. We rented one of the most beautiful apartments in Sutton Place and we gave parties there or went out every evening . . .

'In the end, he was heartsick . . .'

'He told you that?'

'One evening when he'd been drinking, he confessed that some day he would be fed up with being just a puppet . . . You know how his father finished . . .'

Of course I knew. I had known Herbert Sanders well, having often spent the weekend at his home when I was at Yale.

Ray's father was a bookseller, one of a rather special kind. He did not have a bookstore in the city. He lived in a house of the purest New England style on the road to Ansonia, and on the ground floor the walls of every room were entirely lined with books.

People came to see him not only from New Haven, but from Boston, New York, even farther away, in addition to which he received many mail orders.

He was in correspondence with most countries in the world, keeping abreast of everything being written in the fields of palaeontology, archaeology and the arts, in particular the area of prehistoric art.

He had two other obsessions: works on Venice and books on gastronomy, and he prided himself on having more than 160 such titles on his shelves.

A curious man, whom I can still see: young, distinguished, with a smile both ironic and kind.

His first wife, the mother of his two sons, had left him to marry a wealthy landowner in Texas. He had lived alone for a few years, acquiring the reputation of a skirt-chaser.

Then, suddenly, he had married a Polish woman whom no one knew, a gorgeous twenty-eight-year-old.

He was fifty-five. Three months after his marriage, one evening when his wife was out, he had shot himself in the head, among all his books, leaving no note, no explanation.

'Now do you see what I mean?' said Mona.

I refused to accept that revelation. Ray had to remain the man I had imagined, hard on himself and on others, cold and ambitious, the strong man on whom I had taken revenge against all the strong men on this earth.

I did not want a Ray disgusted with money and success.

'You must be mistaken, Mona . . . I'm sure that Ray was happy . . . When people have a few drinks, you know, they tend to dramatize things . . .'

She looked at me as though debating whether to believe me or not.

'He was starting to have had enough,' she insisted. 'That's why he was drinking more and more. I began drinking with him . . .'

She added, hesitantly, 'Here, I didn't dare, on account of Isabel . . .'

She bit her lip, as if afraid she had wounded me.

'You find Isabel forbidding?'

'Don't you? Ray thought so, too. He admired you . . .'

'He admired me, you say?'

'He said you'd chosen your life wisely and well, that you had no need to numb yourself, to go out every evening, to let yourself get carried away in affairs . . .'

'He wasn't making fun of me?'

I was dumbfounded. The reversal was complete.

'According to him, a man able to marry Isabel, to live with her day after day . . .'

'Why? Did he tell you why?'

'Don't you understand?'

She was amazed by my innocence, and I abruptly understood Mona's attitude towards me during those past few days. For her, the strong man was not Ray, it was me.

And, quite naturally, it was my protection she had sought. When she looked at me, from deep in her armchair, when she brushed me with her shoulder, it was not simply a sensual thing.

'I've often observed the two of you, Donald . . . With Isabel, you cannot cheat. You can't behave beneath yourself, either, not even for a moment. She's an extraordinary woman, and you have to be extraordinary to live by her side . . .'

I was so confused and upset that it took me more than two hours to fall asleep later that night.

'Ray, he had his ups and downs, like everyone . . . Say, you're not going to drop me, are you, now that he's gone?'

'But Mona, on the contrary, I ask only . . .'

I almost jumped up to rush over and take her in my arms. I was troubled, elated, beside myself.

'Shh . . . She's coming . . .'

Out in the snow we could see the little Volkswagen I had bought my wife for running her local errands. From a distance, I watched Isabel come out of the garage, carrying her bag of groceries: serene, clear complexion with always a touch of pink at the cheekbones, and the blue eyes, those eyes that refused all lying, all cheating.

I would have to rethink everything. Ray had admired me. That was the most staggering news.

Mona admired me, too; she had just admitted it in her own way. And I, poor fool, who that first night had not dared to reach out over the floor to touch the hand that held me so tightly!

What Mona did not know, when she was talking about my relationship with Isabel, was that I had been released. I, too, had admired my wife. I had even been afraid of her, afraid of a frown, of a passing shadow in her limpid eyes, of a mute judgement.

Because she has never said anything unpleasant to me. She has never reproached me.

I must have had occasion to be disagreeable, unjust, ridiculous, what have you, towards her or our children.

Not one word. Her smile never faded. There were only her eyes. And no one would have seen anything there. Her eyes remained as serene and clear as ever.

What would Mona have thought if I had confessed: 'It's not a woman I married, it's a judge . . .'

Wasn't that what Ray had felt, and hadn't he pitied more than admired me? Unless he had been completely fooled.

He'd believed that I had married Isabel because I was a strong man, capable of accepting the challenge.

On the contrary. With her, I kept living in my mother's skirts. I was still a schoolboy. I remained a Boy Scout.

Too bad for Ray. I did not regret a thing, except that he was depriving me of some guilt. I wanted to have killed him, to have desired his death and helped fate along insofar as I could.

If Ray hadn't even struggled, if he had accepted death with relief, the tragedy I had experienced that night on my bench, in the barn, no longer made any sense.

I needed my revolt to remain total, of my own free will.

I was not a sheep, as people thought. I was cruel, cynical, capable of allowing my best friend to die without holding out my hand to him.

And while he was dying quietly in the snow, with one leg twisted, I was smoking cigarettes and thinking of all the times he had unwittingly humiliated me . . . And not just him! . . . There was Isabel, too . . . The two images blended together a little in my mind . . .

The funeral procession had to slow down two or three times. I tried to see Mona's car, beyond the ones between us.

Was I in love with Mona? I was now able to consider questions frankly, without lying to myself, without cheating.

The answer was no. Not in love. Even if it had suddenly become possible, I would not have married her. I did not want to live with her day and night, either, to link my life with hers.

What I wanted, what would happen soon, was to make love with her.

Not tenderly. Not passionately. Who knows? Perhaps standing up, like Ray and Patricia at old Ashbridge's house.

I wanted to take a female, like that, in passing, and in my eyes, Mona was a real female.

We arrived at the cemetery. The cars followed a number of paths in that metropolis for the dead until we reached a new section, on the hill.

There was snow everywhere. The evergreens looked like Christmas trees. No one was wearing boots, so we were all stomping our feet while the coffin was brought up.

The minister was brief. There were no other speeches. The Miller brothers slipped into the first row, because of the photographers; going closer to Mona, I lightly supported her elbow.

Bob Sanders noticed. He was a head taller than I and so looked down on me, with what I took to be haughty disdain.

A few days earlier I would have been ashamed, crushed. That day, I didn't care. Neither did I care that my wife was watching me in some surprise, doubtless caught off guard by the audacity of my gesture.

We headed for the cars. I was walking next to Mona, whose arm I still supported as if she needed it, whereas she was perfectly calm. Bob Sanders strode up to catch her, ignoring my presence.

'I must say goodbye now, because my plane leaves in less than two hours . . . If you need anything at all, if there are formalities to complete, here is my address in Bonn.'

He handed her a card he'd had ready, which she slipped into her purse.

'Take care of yourself, then . . .'

He shook her hand almost militarily and went on ahead. His car was the first to leave the cemetery.

'He doesn't seem to like you . . .'

He had avoided acknowledging me.

'No . . . I suppose he's imagining things.'

Isabel came up to us.

'Are you going back to New York alone, Mona?'

'Why wouldn't I?'

'Won't it be too painful for you to return to an empty apartment?'

'The maid, Janet, is waiting for me . . .'

Isabel looked at me. It was as if she had given me a hint. I could have offered to accompany Mona and come home that evening by train.

I did not even invite her to have a bite to eat with us. On the other hand, just when she was about to get into her Lincoln, I kissed her on both cheeks, gripping her arms rather hard.

'Goodbye, Mona.'

'Goodbye, Donald. Thank you . . . I suppose I'm going to need you for the formalities, the questions about the estate, and so on?'

'Simply call me at my office.'

'Goodbye, Isabel . . . Thank you, too . . . Without you, I don't know what would have become of me.'

They kissed. One of the Miller brothers rejoined me after Mona's car had driven away.

'You're her lawyer?'

'I suppose so . . .'

'There'll be complicated questions to answer. Might I have your telephone number?'

I handed him one of my cards.

Isabel and I found ourselves alone in the Chrysler.

'Were you thinking of having lunch along the way?'

'No. I'm not hungry.'

'Neither am I.'

I was at the wheel, she was beside me, as usual, and her three-quarter profile was at the right edge of my vision.

We drove for a good fifteen minutes in silence before Isabel spoke.

'How do you think it all went?'

'The burial?'

'Yes . . . I don't know what was bothering me . . . It was as if there were no cohesion, no order . . . I didn't feel any emotion. I don't think anyone did, not even Mona . . . It's true that it hasn't sunk in yet . . .'

Lighting a cigarette, I said nothing.

'The hardest moment will be when she gets home . . .'

I still kept quiet. Now she was the one who felt the need to break the silence.

'I wondered if you should have gone along with her . . .'

'She'll get along just fine on her own.'

'Will you be taking care of the estate?'

'She asked me to. The Millers want to be in touch with me as well.'

'Do you think she'll have enough to live on?'

'More than enough, I'm sure.'

Was I strong? Was I weak? Was I clever? Was I naive? Was I cruel? Was I cowardly? They were the ones trying to find out, even Isabel, who no longer understood and had to puzzle over why, after the business with the cigarette butts, I was not acting more humble, if not scared.

At the house, we settled for a sandwich in the kitchen. It was three o'clock.

'Are you going out?' I asked.

'I'll be leaving soon to do my shopping.'

I, at least, found it a little odd to be alone together in the house. In so few days, I had lost that habit and wondered how we would behave living in tandem.

I went to the office. Higgins was waiting for me.

'I hope you snagged the Sanders estate?'

'I will certainly help Mona Sanders with my advice, but in a private capacity and without charge.'

Higgins made a face.

'Too bad . . . That must be a big haul . . .'

'I have no idea. On the other hand, it's possible that the Miller brothers will engage me to dissolve the company, and that would be different.'

'Everything went well?'

'The way it usually does . . .'

I would have been hard put to describe what had happened at the cemetery, for the good reason that I'd been distracted by my thoughts, preoccupied only with Mona. Once in my office, I almost picked up the phone to call her to ask if she had arrived home all right, mostly to hear her voice.

And yet, once again, I was not in love. I know that is hard to understand, but maybe I'll manage to explain myself.

I worked for two full hours, on an estate, as it happened. The *de cujus* – the dear departed – had taken such careful precautions to avoid taxes that it was almost impossible to establish the value of the assets and divide them among the heirs. I had been studying the file for several weeks.

I dictated several letters to Helen while asking myself why, before her marriage, I had not thought of flirting with her. I looked at pretty girls, of course, including the wives of certain of my friends. Occasionally I desired them. But that desire remained, so to speak, theoretical.

It was forbidden. By what? By whom? I didn't ask myself the question.

I was married. There was Isabel, with her eyes of such limpid blue and her bearing, so calm and relaxed.

Isabel and our daughters. I was fond of our girls, Mildred and Cecilia, and when Mildred was the first to leave us for boarding school, I had missed going to kiss her goodnight in her bed.

Now, except for two weekends a month, I had no more occasion to go upstairs. Mildred was fifteen.

If she were to marry young, in three or four years, five at the most, it would mean the first bedroom to remain empty in the house.

Cecilia's turn would follow, for time was passing ever more quickly. The last five years, for example, seemed shorter to me than a single year when I was between ten and twenty.

Is that because the recent ones were less full?

I dictated. I thought. I looked at Helen, debating whether she was already pregnant and if, in that case, we would find a replacement. Ray had slept with his secretary. He'd slept with all the women who came within reach.

And he was the one Mona felt sorry for. Not finding what he had hoped for in life had demoralized him. So he drank and chased women . . . Poor Ray!

Did Helen realize that it was a new man she had before her? Did Higgins? Would all those I would be meeting discern that they were looking at a new Donald Dodd?

My actions, my attitudes, had not changed. Nor had my voice, of course. But the look in my eyes? Was it possible that my eyes had remained the same?

I went to stand before the bathroom mirror. My eyes are blue, too, a darker blue than Isabel's, with brown flecks, while hers are really the colour of a springtime sky when there is no humidity in the air.

I made fun of myself.

'Well, that did you a lot of good! What are you going to do now?'

Nothing, keep going. Sleep with Mona, of course, without that making any real difference.

Saturday morning, or Friday evening, Isabel or I, or both of us, would go and pick up the girls in Litchfield. We would present, in the car, the image of a united family.

Except that I no longer believed in the family. I no longer believed in anything. Not in myself, not in other people. Basically, I no longer believed in mankind and I was beginning to understand why Ray's father had shot himself in the head.

Who knows if that might not happen to me some day? It was a comfort to have a revolver in the night table drawer.

On the day when I will have had enough of struggling in the void, one squeeze of the trigger – and it's over.

Isabel would manage quite well with the girls, and they would receive a handsome insurance payout.

No one could read those thoughts on my face. You get so used to people that you keep seeing them the way you saw them for the first time.

Did I, for example, notice that Isabel was past forty and that her hair was starting to turn grey? I had to make an effort to convince myself that we had both passed the midpoint in life and would swiftly become old folks.

Wasn't I already an old man to my daughters? Would they ever have imagined that I wanted to make love to a woman like Mona? I bet they told themselves that we no longer made love, their mother and I, and that that's why they don't have a whole bunch of brothers and sisters.

I went home and found Isabel busy cooking. She was looking down, and I touched her cheek with my lips, as usual, then went to change my jacket for an old one I wear at home, of soft tweed with leather elbow patches.

I opened the liquor cabinet and yelled, 'Do you want one?'

She knew what that meant.

'No, thanks . . . Or, just a weak one . . .'

I made a weak Scotch for her and poured one a lot stronger for myself.

She joined me in the living room. She was wearing the flowered housedress she had adopted for domestic chores.

'I haven't changed, yet.'

I held out her glass.

'Here's to you . . .'

'And here's to you, Donald . . .'

I thought I heard a special solemnity in her voice, a kind of message.

I preferred not to look at her eyes, for fear of seeing something different there. I went to sit in my armchair in the library, and she went back to work.

What had she thought when she found the cigarette butts? When she had gone out to the barn, didn't she know that she would find them, or at least some trace of me?

What had made her suspect that when I'd left the house to look for Ray I'd had no intention of battling against the blizzard?

She hadn't seen me change course, the night had been too dark. She would not have been able to hear me shouting because of the wind.

At the moment when I stepped outside, even I was uncertain . . . I had only veered off after taking a few steps.

Did she know that I had been a coward? Because that's what it was, at the beginning. An insuperable physical cowardice. I had been at the end of my strength and needed to escape that ordeal at any cost.

Could she have guessed that? Only on the bench did I understand that I was glad that Ray had disappeared and would probably die, unless he found his way again through some miracle.

Had she also understood? And if so, what were her feelings towards me? Contempt? Pity? I'd seen nothing like that in her eyes. Nothing but curiosity.

Another, wilder idea occurred to me. Isabel had read Olsen's mind, which explained some of her questions, but Olsen didn't really know me and thought like a policeman.

The lieutenant had looked at us in turn, Mona and me, asking himself if there were any ties between us. Of that I'm certain. I would bet that he made discreet inquiries. Well, during the Ashbridges' party it so happened that I was never near Mona.

Does Isabel imagine that Mona and I meet secretly?

I go to New York about once a week and spend the day there. Sometimes I spend the night. Ray was often off travelling, because his agency has offices in Los Angeles and Las Vegas.

When she saw me come back to the house alone, did my wife think, even for an instant, that I had taken advantage of that nightmarish storm to get rid of Ray?

Now that I think back coolly, it doesn't seem impossible. I truly believe that if she were to learn that I had killed a man, she would not show any more reaction but would go on living with me and looking at me as she does: with curiosity, hoping to understand.

We ate alone together in the dining room with the two silver candelabras on the table as usual, each with its two red candles. It's a tradition with her. Her father, the surgeon, was somewhat fond of display.

In my home, above the printing press and the offices of the *Citizen*, we lived much more simply.

Speaking of which, my father had not called me to ask for details about Ray's accident, even though he still published the weekly paper in Torrington, one of the oldest newspapers in New England, having lasted over a hundred years.

He'd lived alone since the death of my mother. He had returned to his bachelor habits and when not eating at the restaurant across the street, where he had his table, he liked to fix his own meals. The woman who cleaned the offices every morning would go upstairs to tidy things there and make his bed.

We lived only around thirty miles from each other, yet I hardly went to see him more than once every two or three months. I would enter his glass-walled office, where he worked in his shirt-sleeves. He would look up from his papers, appearing surprised to see me.

'Hello, Son . . .'

'Hello, Father . . .'

He would continue writing, or correcting proofs, or telephoning. I would sit in the only available armchair, which had been in the same place when I was a child.

'Are you content?'

'Everything's fine, yes . . .'

'Isabel?'

He had a soft spot for her, even though she intimidated him a little. Several times, he had joked to me:

'You didn't deserve a woman like her . . .'

To which he invariably added, dutifully:

'No more than I deserved your mother . . .'

She had died three years earlier.

'Your girls?'

He was never really sure about their ages and thought of them as much younger than they were.

He was seventy-nine. He was tall and thin, stooped. He'd been stooped, skinny, with a true gleam of malice in his little grey eyes for as long as I'd known him.

'The office?'

'I'm not complaining . . .'

He looked out of the window.

'Say! You've got a new car . . .'

He'd kept his for more than ten years. True, he hardly used it. He edited the *Citizen* practically by himself, and his rare collaborators were volunteers.

A woman in her sixties, Mrs Fuchs, whom I had known for ever as well, took care of soliciting advertising.

My father printed business cards, announcements, prospectuses, catalogues for the local stores. He had never sought to expand his business, which was, on the contrary, slowly shrinking.

'What are you thinking about?'

I looked up, as if caught out. Force of habit!

'My father . . . It occurred to me that he hasn't called us . . .'

Isabel no longer had her father or mother, only two brothers, both living in Boston, and one married sister in California.

'I'll have to go and see him one of these mornings.'

'You haven't been there in over a month . . .'

I resolved to go to Torrington. It would interest me to see my father and our house again, with my new eyes.

Back in the library, I hesitated between my paper and the television. I finally opened the paper and fifteen minutes later, while I listened to the hum of the dishwasher, Isabel joined me.

'Don't you think you should call Mona?'

Was it a trap? She seemed sincere, as always. Would she have been capable of insincerity?

'Why?'

'You were her husband's best friend. She probably doesn't have any real friends in New York, and Bob Sanders flew home without bothering to stay a single day more . . .'

'Bob is like that.'

'She must feel lonely in that big apartment. Will she be able to keep such a big place?'

'I don't know.'

'Did Ray have money?'

'He earned lots of it . . .'

'He also spent lots of it, didn't he?'

'I suppose . . . His share of Miller and Miller must represent a tidy sum.'

'When do you plan to go and see her?'

It was not an interrogation. She was speaking unaffectedly, as a woman would to her husband.

'Give her a call. Believe me, it will do her good . . .'

I knew Ray's number by heart because I used to see him now and then when I was in the city. I dialled the number and listened to the phone ring a rather long time.

'I don't think there's anyone home.'

'Unless she's gone to bed . . .'

At the same instant, I heard Mona's voice.

'Hello . . . Who's calling?'

'Donald.'

'It's kind of you to call me, Donald. If you knew how lost I feel here . . .'

'That's why I phoned. It was Isabel's idea.'

'Be sure to thank her for me.'

I thought I heard a hint of sarcasm in her voice.

'If you weren't so far away, I'd ask you to come and spend the evening with me . . . Good old Janet does what she can . . . I wander around from room to room without knowing where to go . . . Has that ever happened to you?'

'No.'

'You're lucky . . . This morning was awful. The procession that took for ever, then those people, at the cemetery . . . If you hadn't been there . . .'

So, she had noticed that he had taken her arm.

'I could have just collapsed in a heap, from weariness . . . And that big pompous Bob who greeted me so ceremoniously before dashing off to the airport . . .'

'I know.'

'Did the Millers speak to you?'

'They asked me if I would be handling your affairs.'

'What did you tell them?'

'That I would help you insofar as I could . . . You should understand, Mona, that I don't want to impose myself. I'm only a small-town lawyer . . .'

'Ray considered you a first-rate attorney.'

'There are a lot more clever ones than I in New York . . .'

'I'd like it to be you . . . Unless Isabel . . .'

'No. She would not see any problem, on the contrary.'

'Are you free Monday?'

'What time?'

'Whenever you want. You'll have two hours of driving . . . Would eleven o'clock be all right?'

'I'll be there . . .'

'Now I'm going to do what I already wanted to do at five o'clock this afternoon: swallow two sleeping pills and go to bed. If only I could sleep for two days . . .'

'Goodnight, Mona.'

'Goodnight, Donald. Until Monday . . . Thank Isabel again for me.'

'I will, right away.'

I hung up.

'Mona says thank you.'

'What for?'

'First off, for everything you did for her. Then, for letting me handle the estate.'

'Why ever would I oppose that? Have I ever objected to you handling some business matter?'

It was true. I had to laugh. That wasn't like her. She never allowed herself to express an opinion. At most, from time to time, in certain cases, a look of approval or, on the contrary, a slightly vague look, which in itself constituted sufficient warning.

'You're going to New York on Monday?'

'Yes.'

'By car?'

'That will depend on the weather. If they forecast more snow, I'll take the earliest train . . .'

There. It was simple. We were chatting like a normal couple, quietly, with ordinary words. Anyone looking on and listening would have taken ours for a model marriage.

Well, Isabel considered me a coward or a murderer, take your pick. And I – I had decided that on Monday, I would cheat on her with Mona.

The house was purring along as usual, because it was a living thing, perhaps because it was very old and had sheltered so many human lives. The rooms, with time, had grown larger. Windows had been changed into doors. Dividing walls had been built, others torn down. Barely six yards from our bedroom, a swimming pool had been cut into the rock.

The house breathed. Now and then the furnace could be heard starting up in the basement. At times a radiator clanked; at others, the wood panelling of a room or one of the beams would creak. Until December, we'd had a cricket chirping in the fireplace.

Isabel opened her paper and wiped off her glasses, because for several years she has needed glasses to read. They made her eyes different, less sure of themselves, not as clear, as if they were frightened.

'How is Higgins?'

'He's fine.'

'Has his wife recovered from the flu?'

'I didn't ask him . . .'

We were gently webbing ourselves in for the rest of the evening, and I had lived like this for seventeen years.

# 5.

It happened, just as I had expected, and I don't think Mona was surprised. I'm even almost sure that she was expecting it, that she was hoping for it, which doesn't mean that she is in love with me.

Before that, Isabel and I had had the traditional weekend with our daughters.

The two of us had gone to get them in Litchfield, without dodging the fifteen-minute conversation with Miss Jenkins, who has small, glittering black eyes and who sputters when she talks.

'If only all our pupils could be like your Mildred . . .'

To be honest, I detest schools and especially all those occasions when parents are reunited with their children. First of all, you see yourself again at every age, which already creates a certain uneasiness. Then you remember, in spite of yourself, the first pregnancy, the infant's first cry, the first baby clothes and finally the day when you take the child to nursery school and leave by yourself.

The years are marked, like stages, with the distribution of prizes, with vacations; traditions are created, which you imagine are immutable. Another child is born, who goes through the same rites, has the same teachers.

You find yourself with a daughter of fifteen, another of twelve, and you've become a man on the decline.

As in that song about Little Jimmy Brown: the bells of birth, the bells of marriage, the bells of burial. Then it starts again with others.

Mildred had hardly got into the car before asking:

'Can I spend the night at Sonia's, Mommy?'

It's always their mother they ask for permission, as if I didn't count. Sonia is the daughter of Charles Brawton, a neighbour who is vaguely our friend.

'Did she invite you?'

'Yes. There's a little party, tomorrow evening, and she insisted that I should sleep over . . .'

Mildred has a face so delicious looking that you'd like to eat it right up. Her complexion is fair like her mother's, but sprinkled with freckles on her nose and under her eyes. She's in despair over them, when they are what give her such charm. Her features are still rather childlike, and her body as well, which resembles a doll's.

'What do you think, Donald?'

I must admit that Isabel never fails to ask my advice. But if I had the misfortune to refuse, I'd set the children against me, so I've always said yes.

'Then what about me!' exclaimed Cecilia. 'I'm going to be left alone in the house?'

Because being there with us, that's being alone! Everyone praises the family, togetherness among parents and children. Cecilia is twelve and is already talking about solitude.

It's true. I was like that at her age. I remember dreary, interminable Sundays with my parents, especially when it rained.

'We'll invite one of your friends over . . .'

So, we parents call one another up. We arrange exchanges.

'Could Mabel come and spend the weekend at our house?'

Sunday morning at eleven, the four of us gathered together again to attend church. There as well, you can see people growing older from year to year.

'Is it true that your friend Ray died in our garden?'

'It's true, dear.'

'Will you show me the place?'

We did not show it to her. With children, we act as if death did not exist, as if only other people, strangers, those outside the family or the small circle of friends, pass away from life into death.

No matter. All that isn't important. What's odder is that Cecilia suddenly said, while we were having Sunday breakfast, 'Are you sad, Mommy?'

'Not at all . . .'

'Is it because of what happened to Ray?'

'No, dear . . . I'm the same as always.'

Both girls look more like their mother than like me, but Cecilia has something different about her. Her hair is almost brown, her eyes are hazel, and, when she was still quite little, she was already saying things that surprised us.

She must think a lot, have an inner life we don't suspect.

'Are you both taking us back?'

'Ask your father . . .'

I said yes. We drove them back Sunday night. We had hardly seen them, in the end.

I watched television. I'd be hard put to say what Isabel did. She is always busy.

Our cleaning lady came back to work. Her name is Dawling. Her husband is the local drunk, the true, complete drunk, who gets into fights every Saturday night in bars and is found sleeping on a sidewalk or next to a road.

He has tried every kind of job and been fired from every one of them. For a short time, he has been raising pigs in a hut he built from old planks at the bottom of his property. The municipality is trying to stop him, because everyone complains about it.

They have eight children, all boys, who all resemble their father and are the terror of the local countryside. People call them the Redheads, without distinguishing one from another, and most of them go around in pairs, because Mrs Dawling almost always has twins.

Those folks form a band, a clan that lives on the outskirts of the community, which allows only poor Mrs Dawling in, as a cleaning lady. She rarely speaks. Her lips are thin, and she looks at everyone with a contemptuous eye. She's willing to work for hire, but she still has her doubts.

'Do you think you'll stay overnight in New York? Do you want me to pack you a suitcase?'

'No . . . I'll almost certainly be through before evening . . .'

Her eyes are beginning to irritate me. I no longer know exactly what they mean. It isn't irony, yet they seem to say:

'I know you, ha! . . . I know everything. Try as you may, you'll not hide a thing from me . . .'

On the other hand, there is curiosity as well in her gaze. It's as if she were constantly speculating about how I will react, what I will do.

She has before her a different man and is perhaps not certain of having explored all his possibilities.

She knows I'm going to New York to see Mona. Didn't my wife sense, while she was here with us, that I wanted her? Doesn't she suspect what is going to happen?

She is careful not to show any jealousy. She is the one who advised me, Thursday evening, to call Sutton Place. She is the one, this Sunday evening, who offered to pack my things, as if it were understood that I would spend the night in New York.

Sometimes I wonder if she isn't pushing me. But why? To keep me from rebelling? To save whatever is still left to save?

She definitely knows that for a week now we have been strangers. Strangers who live together, eat at the same table, undress in front of each other and sleep in the same room. Strangers who talk together as husband and wife.

Would I still be able to make love with her? I don't think so.

Why? Something broke while I was on the red bench in the barn, smoking cigarettes.

Mona has nothing to do with it, no matter what Isabel believes.

The sky was overcast, Sunday night.

'I'll take the train,' I announced.

I rose at six on Monday morning. The sky was a little clearer, but I thought the air smelled like snow.

'Do you want me to drive you to the station?'

She took me there in the Chrysler. The Millerton station is a small wooden building where there are never more than three or four people waiting for the train, a train on which all the passengers know one another by sight. I was greeted by our shoemaker, who was also going to the city.

'Don't bother waiting, you can go on home. I'll call to let you know what train I'll be taking back.'

It did not snow. On the contrary, as we approached New York, the weather cheered up, and the skyscrapers appeared against the purest blue, with a few golden clouds.

I went to have a coffee. It was too soon to go to Mona's place, and after leaving the station I walked along Park Avenue. I, too, could have lived in the city, had an office in one of those glass buildings, lunched with clients or friends, had a cocktail, my day over, in an intimate and dimly lit bar. We could have, in the evening, gone to the theatre, or dancing in a nightclub . . .

We could have . . .

What was it that Mona had said on that point, exactly? That Ray envied me, that I was the stronger of the two, that I had made my choice wisely! A Ray for whom ev erything had been a success and who talked about blowing his brains out!

Rubbish!

Were passers-by really looking at me? I always feel as if people are looking at me, as if I had a birthmark in the middle of my face or were wearing something ridiculous. This feeling was so strong that when I was a child, and then a young man, I would stop in front of shop windows to make certain that I looked completely normal.

At 10.30, I hailed a taxi and went to Sutton Place. I knew the building, the orange marquee, the doorman with the gold-laced coat, the lobby with a few leather armchairs and, to the right, the receptionist's desk.

That man knew me as well.

'For Mrs Sanders, Mr Dodd? . . . Would you like me to announce you?'

'Don't bother, she's expecting me.'

The elevator boy was wearing white cotton gloves. He took me to the twenty-first floor, and I knew at which of the three mahogany doors I should ring.

Janet came to let me in. She's a delectable girl in her black silk uniform, with a pretty embroidered apron, and her face is usually sunny.

I suppose she felt she should wear an expression suitable for the occasion, and she murmured something like, 'Who would ever have believed it . . .'

Relieved of my hat and coat, I was escorted by her into the living room, where I feel almost dizzy every time. It's a vast place, all white, with two bay windows overlooking the East River. I'd known Ray long enough to be certain that the décor did not reflect his own taste.

This room was defiant. He had wanted it to be rich, modern, astounding. The furniture, the paintings on the wall, the sculptures on their pedestals seemed to have been chosen for a film set rather than a place to live in, and the room's dimensions precluded any idea of intimacy.

A door opened in a small room called the boudoir, from which Mona called out:

'Over here, Donald . . .'

I hesitated over whether to bring my briefcase; in the end I left it on the armchair where I'd placed it.

I walked towards her. She was almost ten yards away. She was standing in the doorway, wearing dark blue. She was waiting, watching me approach.

She let me by without holding out her hand and closed the door behind her.

Only then, face to face, did we look into each other's eyes, hesitating. I put my hands on her shoulders and began by kissing her on the cheeks, as in Ray's time. Then, abruptly, without waiting any longer, I crushed her lips with mine, hugging her tightly.

She did not protest, did not stiffen. I saw her eyes staring at me with a certain amazement.

Didn't she know that would happen? Was she surprised at how quickly it had? Or was it my emotion, my clumsiness that were astonishing her?

My entire being began to tremble. I could not take my mouth from hers, my eyes from hers.

I think that deep down I felt like crying.

The blue garment was a peignoir of very supple silk, and I could feel that there was nothing under it but her.

Had she done this on purpose? Had she not had time to dress because I'd arrived ten minutes early?

I murmured, 'Mona . . .'

And she said, 'Come . . .'

We were still in each other's arms as she led me to a couch, on to which we fell at the same moment.

I literally plunged into her, all of a sudden, violently, almost viciously, and for a second there was fear in her eyes.

When I stood up again, she rose swiftly, retying the belt of her peignoir.

'Please forgive me, Mona . . .'

'There is nothing to forgive . . .'

She was smiling at me, still with joy in her eyes but, on her cupid's-bow lips, a hint of melancholy.

'I wanted to so much!'

'I know . . . What can I get you, Donald?'

A small bar was housed in a Louis XV piece. As for the huge bar in the living room, that one didn't hide away at all.

'Whatever you're having . . .'

'Then it will be Scotch . . . Some ice?'

'Please . . .'

'Isabel said nothing?'

'About what?'

'About your trip and our meeting . . .'

'On the contrary . . . She is the one who advised me to call you.'

It was a strange feeling, one I'd never had before. We had just made love savagely and Mona's face still showed some signs of this. Perhaps mine did as well?

Yet the moment we both stood up again we were talking like old friends. We were quite at ease, in mind and body. My eyes must have been shining with delight.

'To us, Donald . . .'

'To us . . .'

'She's an unusual woman . . . I still find her somewhat forbidding . . . It's true that, for a long time, you scared me a little, too . . .'

'Me?'

'That startles you? With most people, you know how to deal with them . . . You quickly discover their weak point . . . You, you don't have one.'

'I've just proved otherwise to you . . .'

'You call that a weak point?'

'Yes, perhaps . . . You know, the night when we slept on the floor, on mattresses, I was hypnotized by your hand, lying on the parquet . . . I had an insane desire to touch it, to seize it. I wonder what would have happened if I had done so . . .'

'In front of Isabel?'

'In front of the whole world, if need be . . . You don't call that a weak point?'

She sat down in an upholstered French armchair and thought for a good while. The peignoir had fallen open over almost all of one thigh, but without bothering either of us. We paid no attention.

'No,' she finally announced.

'I didn't shock you by my brusqueness?'

'I admit that I was disconcerted . . .'

We could talk about it without any fuss, without affectation, like old comrades, like accomplices admitting their weaknesses to each other.

'It had to happen, or we would have spent a ridiculous day thinking of nothing else.'

'Do you feel a bit of affection for me, Donald?'

'A lot.'

'I will need that. I don't want to play the weeping widow, and anyway, that would be distasteful at this moment. I was very fond of Ray, you know that. We had become a couple of true friends . . .'

I was sitting in front of her; here, too, the bay window looked out over the East River, bathed in sunlight.

'When I arrived home Thursday, I almost phoned you . . . The apartment seemed ten times bigger than it actually is and I felt lost in it . . . I was pacing around, touching the furniture, objects, as if trying to reassure myself that they were real . . . I began to drink . . . When you phoned me, that evening, could you tell from my voice that I'd been drinking?'

'I was too keyed up to notice anything. Isabel was watching me . . .'

Mona was watching me as well, silently at first, and then as she said: 'I will never understand her.'

She was smoking, with a dreamy air.

'Do you understand her yourself?'

'No.'

'Do you think she can suffer, that there must be something that could get to her?'

'I don't know, Mona. For seventeen years I've never asked myself that question.'

'And now?'

'I've been pondering it for more than a week.'

'Doesn't she scare you a little?'

'I was used to it . . . I thought it was quite simple . . .'

'You don't think so any more?'

'She watches me live, knows my slightest reactions and doubtless my least little thought . . . She never says a word that might suggest that. She remains quiet and serene.'

'Even now?'

'Why do you ask that?'

'Because she has understood. A woman doesn't make such mistakes.'

'Has understood what?'

'That what just happened would happen sooner or later. You were talking about the night spent on the mattresses. She put you between us on purpose.'

'So as not to seem jealous?'

'No . . . For a test . . . It's even subtler than that, I'd swear . . . To tempt you. To unsettle you.'

I was trying to understand, to see Isabel in this new role.

'At least twice she arranged to leave us alone together and she knew of my desire to throw myself into your arms . . . I needed comfort, to feel someone solid pressed against me.'

'I was no help to you.'

'No . . . At first I thought you were afraid of her . . .'

That's the wrong word. I have never been afraid of Isabel. Only afraid of hurting her, of disappointing her, of appearing inferior to the idea she had formed of me.

As long as my mother was alive, I was afraid of hurting her, and even now, if I feel uncomfortable in my father's printing offices, in Torrington, it's because I wouldn't want him to sense my pity.

He is just a shadow of his former self, as they say. He digs in, through bravado, publishing his paper that no longer has much readership, no matter what the cost.

He keeps up the ironic front that was his hallmark all his life, but he well knows that some day or other he'll have to be taken to the hospital, unless he falls dead in his bedroom or his office.

Can I let him see my fears? And see that each time I leave him I wonder if I'll see him alive again?

Mona checked the time on a small gilt clock.

'I'd bet that by now she knows exactly what just happened . . .'

She kept coming back to Isabel, who preoccupied her, and I asked myself why.

If it had been anyone else, I would have thought that she was hoping to see me get a divorce in order to marry her. That idea put a small knot in my throat, and I rose to top up the glasses.

'I didn't shock you, did I, Donald?'

'No.'

'You still love her, right?'

'No.'

'But you did love her very much?'

'I don't think so.'

She drank her Scotch in smaller sips than the first one, still watching me.

'I feel like kissing you,' she murmured finally, as she rose.

I stood up as well. I put one arm around her and, instead of leaning in for a kiss, I put my cheek against hers, staying like that a long time, watching the landscape outside the windows.

I was very sad.

*

Then that sadness changed into a gentler emotion, in which only a vague bitterness remained.

Leaving my embrace, she said, 'I'd really better get dressed before lunch . . .'

I watched her move towards what I knew was the bedroom. I was resigning myself to sitting with the paper while waiting for her, and my disappointment must have shown on my face because she added, in a perfectly natural way:

'If you'd rather come along . . .'

I followed her into the room, where one of the beds was unmade. The door to the bathroom was open, and some water on the tile floor told me she had taken her bath shortly before my arrival. She sat down at the dressing table and began by brushing her hair before applying make-up.

I followed her movements, the light reflected on her skin, with wonderment. I know that we had just made love, but it was almost more precious to be admitted like this into her feminine intimacy.

'You amuse me, Donald . . .'

'Why?'

'One would think this was the first time you'd ever watched a woman at her dressing table.'

'It is . . .'

'But Isabel . . .'

'That's not the same thing.'

I have rarely seen Isabel sitting at hers, which holds only essential things instead of all the small bottles and jars I saw on Mona's.

'You won't mind lunching here with me? I've asked Janet to prepare us a nice little meal.'

I remember two young lions, at the zoo, who were rolling around gently together with perfect confidence. That was about the feeling I had there with Mona.

When she rose, it was to get some underwear from a wardrobe. She did not hide to take off her peignoir and when naked she was not provocative either. She dressed as naturally as if she had been alone, and I did not miss a single one of her movements, her positions.

Was it still true that I was not in love with her? I think so. I had no thought of living with her, of joining my fate to hers the way I once had with Isabel.

I saw Ray's untouched bed without discomfort; it evoked no disagreeable image for me.

There were two other bedrooms in the apartment, I knew. I had once slept in the guest room when I had missed my train, and Janet used the other, smaller one, closer to the kitchen.

Strangely, there was no dining room, doubtless because all possible space had been devoted to the living room.

'Is this all right? I'm not overdressed?'

She had selected a black dress of delicate woollen material, which she had perked up with a belt of silver braid. She must have known that black was becoming to her.

'You're perfect, Mona . . .'

'Later, we'll have to talk seriously. I can't imagine what I would do if you weren't here, with all the problems cropping up . . .'

Janet had set a small table near one of the bay windows, and there was a long-necked bottle of Riesling in an ice bucket.

'I must move, find a smaller apartment . . . Actually, neither of us liked this one. For Ray, it was all smoke and mirrors, to impress his clients . . . I also think it amused him to invite people over, see a crowd around him, intrigues forming, guests gradually forgetting their dignity . . .'

She looked at me, suddenly serious.

'By the way, I've never seen you drunk, Donald . . .'

'Yet I was so in your presence: Saturday evening, at the Ashbridges' party . . .'

'You were drunk?'

'You didn't notice?'

She paused.

'Not at the time . . .'

'When?'

'I don't know . . . I'm not sure . . . Don't be angry if I'm mistaken . . . When you returned after going to look for Ray, I thought you seemed . . . different.'

A lobster and some cold meats had been set out on a pedestal table for us to serve ourselves. I'd just felt a rush of blood to my head.

'It was not inebriation,' I said.

'What was it?'

Too bad. My mind was made up.

'The truth is, I never went to look for Ray. I was too exhausted. I was winded from the storm, with the feeling that at any moment my heart would stop beating. I had no chance of finding him in the darkness, with the snow whipping my face and closing my eyes.

'So, I headed to the barn . . .'

She had stopped eating and was looking at me in such amazement that I almost regretted my frankness.

'I sat down on a bench we store there during the winter and I lit a cigarette . . .'

'Did you stay there the entire time?'

'Yes. The cigarette butts were on the ground, by my feet. I smoked at least ten . . .'

She was troubled, but not angry at me. In the end, she reached for my hand.

'Thank you, Donald.'

'For what?'

'For trusting me . . . For telling me the truth. I felt that something had happened, but I didn't know what . . . I even asked myself at one point if you might not have had an argument with Ray.'

'Why would I have argued with him?'

'Because of that woman . . .'

'What woman do you mean?'

'Mrs Ashbridge . . . Patricia . . . When Ray went off with her, you seemed jealous . . .'

I was stunned to learn that she knew all about it.

'Did you catch them?' I asked.

'Just when they were coming out . . . I wasn't following them, it was pure chance that I saw them . . . Weren't you jealous of Ray?'

'Not because of her . . .'

'Because of me?'

She was asking the question without any flirtatiousness. We were really both speaking from the heart. It was not, as with Isabel, a battle fought with our eyes.

'Because of everything. I actually pushed open that door through which you saw them leave . . . I wasn't thinking of anything, I'd drunk more than usual . . . I surprised them at it . . .

'And then, abruptly, like a hot flash goes to your head, I felt terribly jealous of Ray . . .

'At Yale, I was a grind considered much more brilliant than he was, forgive me for saying so myself.

'When he decided to set himself up in New York, I told him that he risked vegetating there a long time . . .

'I went to ground in Brentwood, barely thirty miles from my father's house, as if I feared losing that protection . . . And almost immediately, as if to protect myself further, I married Isabel.'

She listened, bewildered, and raised her glass, pointing to mine.

'Drink . . .'

'I've told you everything. You'll guess the rest, my other thoughts that Saturday . . . Ray got you, became a partner at Miller and Miller . . . And along the way, he could pick up women like Patricia, casually . . .'

She spoke slowly:

'And he was the one who envied you!'

'Do I disappoint you, Mona?'

'On the contrary . . .'

She was moved. Her upper lip was quivering.

'How did you summon the courage to tell me all that?'

'You're the only person to whom I can talk . . .'

'You hated Ray, didn't you?'

'That night, on my bench, yes.'

'And before?'

'I considered him my best friend . . . But I discovered on that bench that I'd been lying to myself.'

'And if you could have saved him?'

'I don't know. I probably would have, unwillingly . . . I'm no longer sure of anything, Mona. You see, in one night, I changed a great deal . . .'

'I'd noticed. Isabel did, too.'

'She figured things out so well that she went to the barn and found the cigarette butts.'

'Did she mention them to you?'

'No. She disposed of them. For fear, I'm sure, that Lieutenant Olsen would discover them.'

'Doesn't Isabel believe that you . . . that you did something else?'

I preferred to speak bluntly.

'That I pushed Ray off the cliff? . . . I don't know. For the last week she's been looking at me as if she didn't recognize me, as if she were trying to understand . . . And you? Do you understand?'

'I think so . . .

'Aren't you disappointed?'

'On the contrary, Donald.'

That was the first time I'd ever felt as if bathed in a warm feminine gaze.

'I was wondering if you were going to speak to me about it . . . I would have been a little sad if you hadn't . . . That took courage.'

'Given where I am now, you know . . .'

'And where is that?'

'I've drawn a line through seventeen years – no, what am I saying, forty-five years of life . . . Everything is in the past . . . Yesterday, in front of my daughters, I was ashamed, because I felt like a stranger. And yet, I will continue to go through the same motions, to say the same things . . .'

'Is that necessary?'

I looked at her. I hesitated. It would have been easy. Since I had erased everything, didn't I have the right to start over differently? Mona was in front of me, solemn, trembling.

That minute was decisive. We were eating, we were drinking Riesling, we had the view of the East River flowing at our feet.

'Yes,' I murmured. 'It is necessary.'

I do not know why. That 'yes', I said it with my throat choked up, looking intently at Mona. I was on the point of . . . No, not yet, but I could have, very quickly, begun to love her. I could have moved to New York as well . . . We could have . . . I don't know if she was wounded. She did not show it.

'Thank you, Donald . . .'

She stood up, shaking the crumbs from her dress.

'Will you have some coffee?'

'Please . . .'

She rang for Janet.

'Where would you like to have it? Here or in the boudoir?'

'In the boudoir.'

This time, I brought my briefcase. Then I walked beside her, slowly, one hand on her shoulder.

'You understand me, Mona, don't you? You feel, as well, that it couldn't work . . .'

She raised her hand to take hold of mine, and again I saw that hand on the floor of our living room, in the light of the flames on the hearth.

I felt relaxed. A little later, I sat down at a small antique table on which I had placed pencil and paper.

'First of all, do you know what your situation is?'

'I don't know a thing. Ray did not talk to me about his business.'

'Do you have any ready money?'

'We have a joint bank account.'

'Do you know how much is in it?'

'No.'

'Did Ray have any insurance?'

'Yes.'

'Do you know what his arrangements were with the Millers?'

'He was a partner, but not a full partner, if I've understood correctly . . . Every year, his percentage share increased.'

'Did he leave a will?'

'Not that I know of.'

'Did you look through his papers?'

'Yes.'

I went with her to the office Ray had set up for himself, and we went through his papers together. We were perfectly at ease with each other, without any reservations. The insurance policy, with Mona as the beneficiary, was for two hundred thousand dollars.

'Have you informed the insurance company?'

'Not yet.'

'Or the bank?'

'No. I've hardly left the apartment since Thursday. Sunday morning only, I went out to walk up and down the sidewalk for some fresh air.'

'May I make a few phone calls?'

I was back in my role as a lawyer and notary. She listened to my calls, impressed by the way things were being so easily arranged.

'Would you like me to go to see the Miller brothers on your behalf?'

'Yes, do that, will you?'

I telephoned the Millers and told them I would be coming over.

'I'll be back to see you in a little while,' I told Mona.

I took my briefcase. In the living room, I turned to her and, quite unselfconsciously, as I expected, she came into my arms and kissed me.

The offices of the Miller brothers comprise two entire floors of one of Madison Avenue's new buildings, near the archbishop's drab grey mansion. In one immense room alone, more than fifty employees were working, each at a desk, with one or two telephones within reach, and I had glimpsed in passing the same bustling scene in the creative department.

They were both there waiting for me, David and Bill, short and fat, so alike that people who did not know them well could not tell them apart.

'We are glad, Mr Dodd, that Mrs Sanders chose you to represent her. If she had not, we would have chosen you, as I told you at the cemetery.'

The office was vast, luxurious, just solemn enough for a consultation this important.

'What can I offer you? Scotch?'

A mahogany panel concealed a bar.

'I suppose you are, loosely speaking, abreast of the situation? Here is our partnership contract, as it was drawn up five years ago.'

It consisted of about ten pages; I simply skimmed through it. A first glance indicated that Ray's share might come to around half a million dollars.

'Here are the latest statements . . . You'll have time to study these documents at leisure and contact us again. When are you going back to Brentwood?'

'Probably tomorrow.'

'Might we have lunch together?'

'I'll phone you in the morning.'

'Before you leave, I would like you to have a look in the office of our poor friend and see if there might not be some papers or personal objects to take with you . . .'

Ray's office was almost as impressive as the one I'd just left, and his beautiful red-haired secretary was working at a table. She rose to shake my hand, although I had the impression that she did not appreciate my visit.

I knew her from having stopped by now and then to pick up Ray at his office.

'Do you know, Miss Tyler, if Ray had any personal papers here?'

'That depends on what you would call personal . . . Take a look . . .'

She opened the drawers, leaving me the task of flipping through the files. On the desk sat a silver-framed photograph of Mona.

'I'd best take that with me, don't you think?'

'I suppose . . .'

'I'll be back tomorrow. If you'd be kind enough to collect his small personal effects . . .'

'There's even a coat in the closet.'

'Thank you.'

I had myself driven to the bank, then to the headquarters of the insurance company. I was liquidating, not only a man's past, but the man himself. I was legally erasing him, the way the Miller brothers were erasing him from their corporate name.

It was six o'clock when I arrived at Sutton Place. Mona opened the door to me, and we kissed as if this had become a ritual.

'Not too tired?'

'No . . . I still have lots to do tomorrow . . . It would be better if you came to the Millers' office with me.'

Without asking, she was pouring our drinks.

'Or do you want . . .'

She was going to ask me again if I preferred the living room or the boudoir.

'You know perfectly well . . .'

We began drinking, both of us, without much talk.

'You're rich, my dear Mona . . . Including the insurance, you're going to find yourself sitting on seven hundred thousand dollars.'

'As much as that?'

She was astonished, but you could tell that the figure meant nothing specific to her.

'May I call home?'

Isabel answered right away.

'You were right . . . I won't be able to come home to Brentwood tonight . . . I saw the Millers, yes, and I have to study the documents they gave me for tomorrow's meeting.'

'Are you at Mona's?'

'Yes, I just got back.'

'Are you planning on staying at the Algonquin?'

That's the old hotel we used when we spent the night in the city. It's in the theatre district, and I was eight the first time I went there with my father.

'I don't know yet.'

'I understand.'

'Is everything fine at the house?'

'There's nothing new . . .'

'Goodnight, Isabel.'

Goodnight, Donald . . . Give my regards to Mona.'

I repeated aloud, turning towards her, 'My wife sends you her regards.'

'Thank her and give her mine . . .'

After I'd hung up, she looked at me questioningly.

I understood that she was thinking of the Algonquin.

'Because of Janet,' I said softly.

'You think that Janet doesn't already know?'

She looked over at the couch.

'Why don't we have dinner in a little restaurant off the beaten track and then come back here to bed?'

She filled the glasses.

'I'll have to get used to drinking less. I drink way too much, Donald.'

Then, after some thought, as if struck by an idea:

'Aren't you afraid Isabel will call you back at the Algonquin?'

I replied with a smile.

'You think she doesn't know, too?'

I wondered if I'd be obliged to sleep in Ray's bed. In the end, we both squeezed into Mona's bed, next to the one left empty.

# *Part Two*

## 1.

Isabel continues to watch me. Nothing else. She does not ask me any questions. She does not reproach me. She does not cry. She does not play the victim.

Life goes on as in the past. We still sleep in the same room, use the same bathtub, eat together and, in the evening, when I haven't brought home work, we read or watch television.

Every two weeks, the girls come for the weekend, and I believe that they don't notice a thing. True, they are more preoccupied by their own personal lives than by ours.

Basically, they have already lost interest in us, at least where Mildred is concerned. The twenty-year-old brother of one of her friends claims a greater share of her attention than we do.

Every day, morning, noon and night, Isabel looks at me with her pale-blue eyes, and it feels like a collision. I wind up no longer knowing what those eyes are saying.

Do they contain a message? Sometimes I wonder.

'Careful, my poor Donald . . .'

No. They don't show enough warmth for that.

'If you think I don't understand what's going on . . .'

She certainly wants to show me that she is lucid, that nothing escapes her, has ever escaped her.

'You're going through a crisis typical of almost all men your age . . .'

If she thinks that, she's mistaken. I know myself. It isn't the infatuation of a man growing old. Besides, I am not in love. Neither am I plunging into some kind of pathological sexuality.

I remain composed, attentive to what is happening inside me and around me and am alone, no doubt, in knowing that there is nothing new in my innermost thoughts, except that I have finally dared to look at them in the light of day.

So, what is it those eyes want to say?

'I pity you . . .'

That is more likely. She has always harboured a need to protect me, or to seem to protect me, just as she imagines that she protects our daughters, that she is the driving force in all the projects she undertakes.

Modest, self-effacing, she is actually the most arrogant woman I have ever met. She never allows the slightest fault to show, none of our little human weaknesses.

'I will always be here, Donald . . .'

That is also there in her eyes: the faithful companion who sacrifices herself to the very end! But in the end, there is something else.

'You imagine that you have freed yourself . . . You think you are a new man . . . In reality, you remain the little boy who needs me and you will never free yourself.'

I don't know any more. I lean now towards one hypothesis, now towards another. I live under her gaze, like a microbe under the microscope, and sometimes I hate her.

Three months have passed since the bench in the barn. The bench is gone, back in its place in the garden, near the cliff, as it happens, from which Ray fell. The last scraps of snow have been absorbed by the warming earth, and the jonquils are sprinkling their yellow accents everywhere.

The first month, I went to New York up to twice a week, staying overnight almost every time, because Ray's estate and the incumbent formalities required much time and effort.

'Where should I call you in the evening if something urgent comes up?'

'At Mona's.'

I'm not hiding away. I am, on the contrary, behaving rather brazenly and when I return from New York I'm glad to smell Mona's scent on my skin.

Bad weather no longer forces me to take the train. I drive my car. There is a parking lot across from her building. Or rather, there was, because as of two weeks ago Mona no longer lives in Sutton Place.

Through friends, she found an apartment on 56th Street, between Madison and Fifth Avenues, in one of those narrow row houses in the Dutch style that are so charming.

The ground floor tenant is a French restaurant that makes a savoury coq au vin. Her apartment is on the fourth floor, much smaller, of course, than the old one.

Warmer and more intimate as well. For the new living room, she used the furniture from the boudoir, including the couch upholstered in golden-yellow silk.

The bed is new, a vast double bed, very low, but the dressing table and French armchair are still the same ones as before.

The dining room will not hold more than six or eight at the table, but Janet has a rather big kitchen and a pretty bedroom.

I don't know which friends found her this apartment. In Ray's time, they frequented many people, entertaining or going out almost every evening.

That is a subject that remains closed to me. As if by agreement, we do not discuss it. I have no idea whom she sees when I'm not in the city and no idea if she has one or several lovers.

It's possible. She loves to make love, without romantic illusions, I would almost say without passion, as friends.

Whenever I arrive, I find her in a peignoir and lead her in the most natural way to the couch on which I entered her for the first time.

Afterwards, she pours our drinks, carries the two glasses into the bedroom and begins her morning ritual.

'How is Isabel?'

She talks to me about her every time I visit.

'She still hasn't said anything yet?'

'She looks at me . . .'

'It's a tactic.'

'What do you mean?'

'By watching you silently, without upbraiding you, she'll wind up giving you a guilty conscience.'

'No.'

'She's counting on it.'

'Perhaps, but if so, she's wrong.'

Mona is intrigued by Isabel and she is the one who is impressed by her personality.

As for me, this is one of the best moments of my day, of my week. She busies herself with her toilette, and I sink with delight into this intimate scene as if into a hot bath.

I know every one of her movements, each expression, the way she purses her mouth to apply lipstick.

When she takes her bath, I follow the water droplets that zigzag along her flushed skin. Because her skin is not pale and tinged with pink like Isabel's, but more golden.

She is quite petite, actually. She weighs nothing.

'Has Lowenstein made up his mind?'

Because we do discuss her business. We even pay a great deal of attention to it. Lowenstein is the decorator who made an offer to buy all the furnishings at Sutton Place, except for the few pieces Mona kept back.

Only the price was still a matter for debate. Now that's settled, and the lease has gone to an actor recently arrived from Hollywood to appear on Broadway.

The negotiations with the Miller brothers are almost completely wound up, and the name of Sanders has long since been scraped off the glass panels where it appeared after Miller and Miller. Only a few details remain to be dealt with.

I never asked Mona what she did with Ray's clothing, his golf clubs, a certain number of personal belongings I no longer see anywhere.

We often go down to the little ground-floor restaurant, where we always choose the same corner. The owner comes over to shake hands. We are treated like a couple, and it amuses us. In the afternoon, I almost always have to rush around everywhere, either for Mona's business or for mine. We arrange to meet later in a bar. We drink martinis because, for the evening cocktail, we have adopted the extra-dry martini.

We do enough drinking, perhaps too much, but without ever being drunk.

'Where shall we have dinner?'

We wander at random, on foot, and sometimes Mona, perched on her high heels, takes my arm. Once, we encountered Justin Greene, from Canaan, one of old Ashbridge's guests, in fact, who was present at that memorable evening. He hesitated to acknowledge us. I turned around at the same moment he did, and he seemed embarrassed.

By now, all Brentwood – indeed, the whole area – must know that I'm conducting an affair in New York. Did he recognize Mona? It's possible, although improbable, because it was the first time she had ever been to that house, and she had hardly made herself conspicuous.

'Was that one of your clients?'

'An acquaintance . . . He lives in Canaan . . .'

'Doesn't it bother you that he saw us?'

'No . . .'

On the contrary! I'd finished with all those people. One day they would certainly realize that although I was still pretending to play the game, I no longer believed in it.

One Saturday, I went to Torrington. It's a placid little town, with only two commercial streets, surrounded by residential neighbourhoods.

To the west, there's a bit of industry, but it's almost artisanal, a watch factory, for example, and another plant, brand new, where they manufacture minuscule components for electronic instruments.

The house where I was born is on the main street, at the corner of a dead end, with a sign saying the *Citizen* in gothic letters. Most of the workers in the printing shop have been with my father for more than thirty years. Everything is antiquated, including the machines that entranced me when I was a child.

Because it was Saturday, the print shop was closed. Nevertheless, my father was in his glass cage and could be seen, in his usual shirt-sleeves, from the street.

He had always worked in that spot, as if to proclaim that the newspaper had nothing to hide.

The door was not locked. I went in. I sat down on the other side of the desk and waited for my father to look up.

'It's you?'

'I'm sorry for not having come by lately . . .'

'It means that you had something else to do. So there's no need to apologize . . .'

That's my father's style. I don't believe he has ever kissed me, not even when I was little. In the evening he would simply offer his forehead, like Isabel. I never saw him kiss my mother, either.

'You're in good health?'

I replied yes, just as it dawned on me that my father had aged a lot in the last few weeks. His neck was so thin that the tendons showed, and his eyes looked a little faded.

'Your wife came by a few days back.'

She had not mentioned that to me.

'She'd come to do some errands, to buy some dishes, I think, from that old thief Tibbits . . .'

A shop that existed already in my day, selling china and silverware. I had known old Tibbits and then his son, now old himself.

When we got married, we bought our set of dishes from Tibbits, and when too many pieces had been broken, Isabel would come to Torrington to replace them.

'Are you still content?'

The relationship between my father and me was so reserved that I never knew how to interpret his questions. He would often ask me if I was content, the way he asked me for news about the health of Isabel and the girls.

But, this time, didn't the question go deeper? Hadn't my wife spoken to him? Hadn't any rumours reached him?

He continued to run his eyes over the proofs, striking out a word and replacing it, in the margin, with another.

Had we ever had anything to say to each other? I stayed there, looking at him, sometimes turning to the street, where the traffic had changed since my childhood. Once, passing cars had been rare, and you could park anywhere.

'How old are you, by the way?'

'Forty-five.'

He nodded, murmuring as if to himself, 'That's young, of course . . .'

He was about to turn eighty. He had married late, after the death of his father, who was already running the *Citizen*. He had begun his career in Hartford and had worked, for only a few months, on a daily paper in New York.

I had a brother, Stuart, who would most likely have taken over the business if he had not been killed in the war. He was more like my father than I was, and I have the impression that the two of them got along well together.

My father and I got along well, too, but without intimacy.

'It's your life, after all . . .'

He was muttering. I hadn't necessarily heard him. Was it better to let the matter drop, to talk about something else?

'Are you referring to Mona?'

My father pushed his glasses back up on his nose and looked at me.

'I didn't know her name was Mona.'

'Isabel didn't tell you?'

'Isabel did not tell me anything . . . She's not a woman who talks about her business, even to her father-in-law.'

There was obvious admiration in his voice. You might have thought that he and Isabel were cut from the same cloth.

'So, who told you that I had a mistress?'

'Everybody, more or less . . . There's talk . . . It seems she's the widow of your friend Ray . . .'

'That's true.'

'The one who had the accident, at your house, the night of the blizzard, right?'

I flushed, because I sensed a vague accusation behind those words.

'I'm not the one putting the two things together, Son . . . It's other people.'

'Which people?'

'Your friends in Brentwood, Canaan, Lakeville . . . Some of them wonder if you'll get divorced and go to live in New York.'

'Certainly not.'

'I'm not asking you the question, but others have asked me, and I've told them that it's none of my business.'

He wasn't reproaching me, either. He seemed not to have any hidden agenda, again like Isabel. He filled his old curved pipe with the burned bowl and lit it slowly.

'Did you come to tell me something?'

'No . . .'

'Did you have anything to do in Torrington?'

'Again, no . . . I just wanted to see you.'

'Would you like to go upstairs?'

He had understood that it was not only him I had come to see, but the house as well, that I was there, in short, to come face to face with my youth.

It's true that I would have liked to go upstairs, to see once more the apartment of former days, where I'd crawled around before I could stand up, and where my mother had seemed like an immense being.

I can just see her eternal apron with tiny checks, the kind they still wore in those days.

No. I could no longer go up there. Not after what my father had just told me.

I could no longer make contact with him as I had obscurely hoped to do, either.

In fact, what had I come to do?

'You know, it must be rather a mess up there, because the cleaning lady doesn't come on Saturday and Sunday . . .'

I imagined the old man alone in the apartment where the four of us had lived. He drew slowly on his pipe, which made a familiar gurgle.

'Time passes, Sonny . . . For everyone, you see. You've gone more than halfway along the path . . . Me, I'm beginning to catch sight of the end . . .'

He was not waxing sentimental about himself, which would not have been in his character. I sensed that he was speaking for me, that he was trying to show me his thoughts.

'Isabel was sitting where you are now . . . When you introduced her to us, your mother and I did not much like her.'

I couldn't help smiling. She was from Litchfield, and in our part of the world those people were considered snobs who thought themselves a cut above the rest of us.

Wide boulevards, lots of greenery, lovely houses and, especially in the morning, men and women out riding horses.

Isabel had had her horse.

'You can be mistaken about people, you see, even when you think you know them. She's a fine woman.'

When my father called someone fine, that was his highest compliment.

'Again, it's your business . . .'

'I am not in love with Mona, and we have no plans for the future.'

He coughed. He had had chronic bronchitis for a few years now and occasionally had painful fits of coughing.

'Please excuse me.'

His physical decline humiliated him. He hated making a spectacle of it before others. I think that's why he would have preferred that we no longer visit him.

'What were you saying? . . . Ah, yes . . .'

He relit his pipe and, while puffing on it, announced, slowly and distinctly:

'In that case, it's even worse.'

I was wrong to have visited my father. I'm certain that I disappointed him. And I was disappointed as well. There was no connection between us, whereas, from the little he told me, I realize that he and Isabel have been keeping up some kind of relationship. When I got into my car, I saw, through the window, that he was watching me leave and probably thinking, as I did, that we had perhaps seen each other for the last time.

During the entire drive home, I kept seeing his worn-out face, his melancholy dignity, and I asked myself questions. Has he really kept his faith to the end and, at the moment of leaving, does he still harbour illusions?

Does he believe in the usefulness of this little newspaper, which fought against injustice a hundred or even sixty years ago but which no longer does anything but flatter people's vanity by reporting on engagements, weddings, parties and other unimportant local events?

He has devoted his life to the *Citizen* as seriously as if he had been fighting for a great cause and he is clinging to the paper until his last breath.

It's what would have happened to my brother if he hadn't died at the front. With small differences, isn't that what happened to me as well, until, on the bench in the barn, I lit a first cigarette?

After a while, I drove more slowly. Lately I've been subject at times to sudden sensations of vertigo. I am not ill. It isn't fatigue, either, because I'm not working any harder than usual.

Age? It's true that I am now conscious of my age, which I'd never thought about, and the sight of my father has reinforced this.

I would have liked to explain something to him, about Mona. I tried. Did he understand that to me she is above all a symbol?

We are not in love. I am not sure that I believe in love, or in any case, in a love that lasts a lifetime.

We join together because it reassures us to feel skin against skin, to live in the same rhythm. That's still the closest, in the union of two beings, that one can be.

We need someone. I needed Isabel, not in the same way. I needed her as a witness, as a guard rail, I'm not sure what, exactly. It's all so far in the past that I myself no longer understand what I was seeking in her and am beginning to hate her.

Her gaze exasperates me. It has become an obsession. When I arrived home, without having mentioned either Torrington or my father, she asked:

'How is he?'

It's easy to figure out, I admit. There are clues. But I constantly feel myself at the end of a string. Wherever I go, whatever I do, it's a little as if she were keeping her eyes fixed on me.

I only go once a week to New York now, because the estate has been taken care of and, even with regard to Mona, I did need an excuse. I must not lapse back into what I was. I could not bear that any more. When you've made certain wrenching discoveries, it's impossible to go backwards.

I need Mona, which is to say her presence, an animal intimacy. I love it when, naked or half naked, she goes about her morning routine without paying attention to me. I love, in bed, feeling her skin against mine.

As for the rest, though, hasn't our experiment been a failure? I've talked about the restaurants where we'd have lunch and dinner, the little bars where we'd have our two late-afternoon martinis.

We were still good friends, of course. We were perfectly at ease with each other. But to tell the truth, I did not feel in communication with her and at times I had to look for something to say. It was the same for her.

Nevertheless, she is everything that I did not possess during those forty-five years, everything I shied away from, out of fear.

The girls have been back. I've been observing Mildred a lot. I love her complexion, the colour of warm bread, and the way she crinkles her nostrils when she smiles. She has begun to wear make-up, not at school, of course, where that must be forbidden, but at home.

Does she imagine that we don't notice? She spent last Sunday afternoon with her friend, the girl who has the twenty-year-old brother. Who will probably be what she'll later call her first love. She has no idea that the memory of those furtive glances, those blushes, those hands brushing against each other as if by chance will pursue her all her life.

She will not be pretty in the usual sense of the word. She isn't beautiful, either.

What kind of man will she meet and what life will she live with him?

I see her as a housewife, one of the women whom I class among those who smell like pastry.

As for Cecilia, I don't know. She remains an enigma, and I would not be surprised if she possesses quite a strong personality. She watches us live, and I'm almost convinced that she does not approve of us, that the only thing she feels for us is a certain disdain.

It's really odd! For years you're so preoccupied with the children that they become the reason for everything you do. The house is arranged for them, along with Sundays, vacations, and one fine day you find yourself face to face, strangers to each other, like my father and me.

I repeat that I was wrong to go and see him. That visit has reinforced a pessimism I'm only too inclined to indulge in when I'm not in New York. And even when I am there, actually, aside from certain moments that could be counted in minutes.

It wouldn't take much to get me talking about a conspiracy. Isabel and my father, for a start! Why did she go to Torrington? Was it so important to replace a few plates, when most of the time there are only two of us at the table? It has been six months since we've invited anyone to the house.

My father claims that Isabel did not talk to him about Mona or me. Fine! I have to believe him. But he, didn't he speak to her about us? Even if he didn't, all they had to do was look at each other.

'So, what's Donald up to?'

She must have smiled, with a smile as pale as the sun after a rain.

'Don't worry about him . . .'

Wasn't she watching over me? Doesn't she keep an eye on me every day, at every hour?

Now here were the locals getting involved, whispering as I pass. They've finally got some disreputable gossip to spread around . . . Donald Dodd, you know, the lawyer whose office is almost directly across from the post office . . . The partner of old Higgins, yes . . . The one who has such a nice, sweet, devoted wife . . . Well, he's carrying on an affair in New York!

Higgins joins in. When I tell him that I'll be going to New York the following day he asks:

'Will you be there for two days?'

'Not this time, no . . .'

Higgins ought to be satisfied, though, because the Miller brothers paid us handsomely indeed for the work I did. I would have done it for nothing, to help Mona. They are the ones who insisted on it.

Warren, our doctor, came to see me at my office to ask me a question about his taxes, because I handle his affairs. He studied me closely while we were chatting, and I suspected that his story about the taxes was simply a pretext.

Wouldn't Isabel have been capable of calling him? Of telling him, for example:

'Listen, Warren . . . I'm worried. For some time now, Donald hasn't been the same . . . His moods have changed. He seems very strange.'

I abruptly looked Warren right in the eye. He's an old friend. He was at the Ashbridges' on 15 January.

'You find me very strange as well, do you?'

He was so startled that he had to catch his glasses.

'What do you mean?'

'Just what I said. For a while now, when I go by, people have tended to turn around and whisper . . . Isabel looks at me as if she were wondering what's happening to me, and I strongly suspect her of having sent you here.'

'Donald, I assure you . . .'

'Am I very strange, yes or no? . . . Do I seem like a man in full possession of his wits?'

'You're joking, aren't you?'

'Not in the least . . . Get this: sometimes, in New York, I meet a woman friend with whom I have sexual relations . . .'

I spoke those words with sarcastic emphasis.

'Does that surprise you?'

'Why would it surprise me?'

'Did you know that?'

'I'd heard it mentioned . . .'

'You see! . . . And what else have you heard?'

He must have been sorry he'd come, he felt so embarrassed.

'I don't really know . . . That you might make certain decisions . . .'

'For example?'

'To go and live in New York . . .'

'To get divorced?'

'Perhaps.'

'Did Isabel talk to you about it as well?'

'No.'

'Have you seen her recently?'

'That depends on what you mean by recently.'

'Within the past month?'

'I believe so . . .'

'Did she go to see you at your office?'

'You're forgetting patient confidentiality, Donald.'

He tried to smile while saying those words as casually as possible. He was getting to his feet, but I did not set him free yet.

'If she went to see you, it wasn't because of her health. She went to talk to you about me, to tell you that she was worried, that I wasn't myself any more.'

'I don't like the turn this conversation is taking.'

'Neither do I, but I'm beginning to be fed up with being an object of curiosity . . . I did not go looking for you. You are the one who came here, under a poor pretext, to peer up my nose, take my temperature . . .

'Are there some tests you'd like me to have? . . . Have you seen enough to reassure my wife? . . . Do I seem very strange to you as well, because I start telling people what's bothering me?

'You're much more Isabel's friend than you are mine . . . All our friends are in the same boat. Isabel is an extraordinary woman, of exemplary devotion, of boundless goodness . . .

'Well, my dear Warren, one doesn't sleep with devotion and goodness. I've been doing that for too long not to be fed up with it. I will go to New York or elsewhere, when I please, no matter what the honourable citizens of this county think of that . . .

'As for Isabel, if she's worried, reassure her: I have no intention of divorcing and of remaking my life elsewhere . . . I will continue to work in this office and go home obediently to the house . . .

'So, do you still find me very strange?'

He shook his head sadly.

'I don't know what's come over you, Donald . . . Have you been drinking?'

'Not yet . . . I'm going to in a moment . . .'

I was beside myself. I don't know why I suddenly became so furious. Especially with poor Warren, who is truly the last person with whom I could be angry. The pill-doctor, as the children call him. In his visits, he lugs along a Gladstone bag that looks like a travelling salesman's case. All one side is kitted out with tubes and flasks and, after listening to his patient's chest, he looks over his collection, selects a flask, takes from it (according to need) two, four, six pills, which he slips into a little envelope.

He has pills of every colour: reds, greens, yellows and rainbow-tinted ones my daughters, when younger, naturally preferred above all others.

'Here . . . You'll take one fifteen minutes before dinner and another before bed. Tomorrow morning . . .'

Poor Warren! I had dumbfounded him, and my anger vanished as quickly as it had come.

'I apologize, Warren . . . If you were in my place, you would understand. As for my mental state, I don't think you need to worry yet. Do you agree?'

'I did not think for an instant that . . .'

'Yes, well, but others have thought so for you. Reassure Isabel . . . Don't tell her that I said to . . .'

'You're really not angry with me?'

'No.'

I wasn't angry with him, but I was troubled, because I wondered if I hadn't just discovered the reason why there was anxiety in my wife's eyes.

She had always been so sure of me, so sure of what she must have considered my equanimity, that she could not believe that I had deliberately changed.

I kept coming back to the cigarette butts she had disposed of. Was it possible that she'd believed that I had pushed Ray?

My trips to New York, my intimacy with Mona, paraded almost cynically after my friend's death – did they not seem like proof to her?

In which case, I had to be of unsound mind. That was the only way for her to explain my attitude.

I had just spoken of drinking. Indeed, I went to have a Scotch in the bar across the way, frequented mostly by truck drivers, where I almost never go.

'Another, please . . .'

Here as well people looked at me, of course, and if Lieutenant Olsen had come in, my attitude would have given him something to think about.

Another one who had his doubts. I was surprised that he hadn't tried again. Was he convinced Ray's death was due to a simple accident?

He must have heard that I was Mona's lover and that we could be seen in New York walking arm in arm.

I did not have a third drink, although I wanted one. I went back across the street to the office.

'Are you going to New York, this week?'

'Why do you ask?'

'Because if you go, I'd ask you to do something for me there . . . What neighbourhood will you be in?'

'Around Fifty-sixth Street . . .'

'It's a document to be registered at the Belgian Consulate, in Rockefeller Center . . .'

'I might be going in on Thursday.'

'Say, you really shook him up, that poor Warren . . . It wasn't my fault, I couldn't help overhearing . . .'

'Do you find me strange, too?'

'Strange, no, but you have changed. To the point that I wondered if you would stay here and if I ought to look for a partner . . . For me, that would be a catastrophe. Do you see me, at my age, training up some youngster? . . . Didn't the Millers offer to bring you in with them?'

'No.'

'Now that surprises me . . .'

I wasn't telling the truth. No, they had not made me a direct offer. They had, however, asked me about my plans, my life in Brentwood, and I had understood where they were going.

They, too, were mistaken about my relationship with Mona. They thought it was a great love affair and imagined that in a few weeks I would be settling in New York to live with her and get married.

Then I would really have stepped into Ray's shoes!

'Anyway, I'm glad you're staying . . .'

From his office, which faces the street, he'd seen me head over to the bar, which wasn't one of my habits.

What does he think, this old fox who looks more like a wily horse trader than a lawyer?

Too bad! Let them think what they want, the whole lot of them, Isabel included, of course, Isabel first of all.

When I got home, she welcomed me with a simpering smile, as if I were unhappy or ill.

It's a game that is beginning to grate on me, and I'll have to get used to it. I ought to decide once and for all to pay no more attention to her expressions.

She plays them like cards, deliberately. They're her secret weapon. She knows I'm trying to understand, that it makes me uneasy, eats away at my assurance.

She deploys an entire range of looks like precision instruments. I might reply to words, but you cannot reply to eyes.

If I asked her, 'Why are you looking at me that way?' she would answer with another question: 'In what way am I looking at you?'

In every way. It changes with the days, the hours. Sometimes her eyes are empty, and that's perhaps the most disconcerting look. She's there. We are eating. I say a few words, to avoid a painful silence.

And she looks at me with absent eyes. She watches my lips move the way one watches the lips of a fish open and close in its bowl.

At other times, on the contrary, her pupils contract, and she stares at me as if asking an anguished question.

What question? Did she still have any, after seventeen years of marriage?

Her attitudes, her poses, her way of holding her head tilted to the left, the hint of a smile hovering about her lips, all that never changed, remained immutable. A statue.

Unfortunately, that particular statue was my wife, and she had eyes.

The most curious thing was, morning and evening, when I leaned down to brush her forehead or cheek with my lips: she did not move, not a twitch.

'Good Morning, Isabel . . .'

'Good morning, Donald . . .'

I might just as well have been putting a dime into the slot of a collection box in church.

I tried not to undress in front of her any longer. It bothered me, just as it bothered me to see her half naked.

For her part, she kept doing it. She did it on purpose. Not immodestly, she had always been very modest. But like an acquired right.

There were only two men in the world before whom she had the right to undress: her husband and her doctor.

Had Warren, after our encounter, called her up? Had he reassured her? Had he told her what had happened?

There were moments when I wanted to make a commotion, like that morning in the office. I restrained myself.

I did not want to give her that satisfaction. Because she would have been satisfied.

Not only was she intelligent, good, devoted, indulgent, what-have-you, but I would have handed her the palm of martyrdom besides!

I really hated her. And I realized that it was not so much her fault, or mine, either. In short, she represented everything I had suffered, the stifling of my whole life, that humility I had imposed on myself.

'Don't put your fingers in your nose . . .'

'You must respect old people . . .'

'Go wash your hands, Donald . . .'

'We don't put our elbows on the table . . .'

Those words, it wasn't Isabel who said them. It was my mother. But for seventeen years, Isabel's eyes had told me exactly the same thing.

I knew I had only myself to blame, since I had chosen her.

And the best part is that I had chosen her on purpose.

To keep an eye on me? To judge me? To prevent me from committing too many stupid blunders?

It's possible. It's hard for me to remember what I was thinking when I met her. I was hesitating, at the time, over joining Ray in New York. I'd also been approached about a job in Los Angeles, and I had been tempted.

What might I have become? What would I have become, without Isabel? Would I have married a Mona?

Would I, like Ray, have earned a lot of money while despising myself to the point of talking about suicide?

I haven't any idea. I prefer not to know, not to ask myself any further questions. I would have liked to draw up a well-organized, neat dossier, without any smudges.

I haven't come close.

And I continue, at my age, to spy on my wife's eyes!

## 2.

The Easter vacation was painful. The weather was splendid: every day the same still-youthful sun and a few gilded clouds in the sky. Beneath the living room windows, the rock garden was crowded with flowers and humming with bees.

In spite of the cool air, the girls swam in the pool, and their mother took two or three dips there. We went on a trip to Cape Cod, where we walked barefoot for a long time on the sand by an almost-unruffled sea.

Deep inside me, I no longer felt like a husband or father. I wasn't anything any more. An empty carcass. An automaton. Even my profession as a lawyer no longer interested me, and I saw too clearly the crookedness of my clients.

I was no better than they were. I hadn't made any attempt to keep Ray from dying in the snow at the foot of the cliff. The question was not to determine if my intervention would have changed his fate. Baldly put, the fact was that I had gone to sit on the red bench in the barn.

And gradually, smoking cigarettes and sheltering from the blizzard, I had felt a physical satisfaction, a warmth in my chest, at the idea that he was dead or dying.

That night, I had discovered that for the entire time I had known him I had never stopped envying and hating him.

I was not the friend and neither was I the husband, the father, the citizen whose roles I had played. It was just a façade. The whited sepulchre of the scriptures.

What was left?

All through this vacation, which left me no escape, Isabel seized the chance to watch me more closely than ever.

It's as if my dismay delights her. It would never occur to her to help me. On the contrary, she manages diabolically to shove my head underwater.

For example, I tried two or three times to strike up a conversation with Mildred. She is beginning to be of an age to tackle serious subjects. Each time, Isabel's look immobilized me.

It seemed to say: 'Poor Donald . . . So, you don't see that you won't get anywhere, that your daughters have no connection with you?'

That connection, they'd had it when they were little. They had turned more readily to me than to their mother.

What image do they have of me now? I don't count any more. When they ask my advice, they don't wait for my answer.

I'm the fellow who spends his days in an office to earn the necessary money, a fellow who's growing old, whose face is beginning to look gaunt, who no longer knows how to laugh or play.

Does Isabel realize that she's running a risk? It's possible. I admit that I no longer know. I've had just about enough of interpreting her looks and seeing her staring at me.

With the children, she is playful, full of bright ideas. Every morning, she was the one who came up with an agreeable activity for the day. Agreeable for her and the girls, of course.

We made several excursions, including two hikes in the mountains. I hate excursions, picnics, long walks in Indian file during which you automatically pull up wild flowers along the path.

Isabel is radiant. At least when she's talking to our daughters. As soon as it's me she's looking at, me she's talking to, she turns back into a wall.

Does she intend to push me to the breaking point? She seems to want to go to the very limit and then, perhaps, she'll hold out her hand to me, murmuring:

'Poor Donald . . .'

I am not poor Donald. I am a man, fully a man, but that is something she will never admit.

The children must have noticed that tension. I sensed a certain wariness, a certain disapproval in my daughters, especially when I pour myself a drink.

And now, each time I offer Isabel a Scotch, she just happens to reply primly:

'No, thanks.'

I'm obliged to drink alone. I did not overdo it a single time. There has never been the slightest slippage in my behaviour. No stumbling over words, no nervous excitement.

My daughters still look at me, when I have a glass in my hand, as if I were committing a sin.

This is new. They've often seen us have a drink or two, their mother and I. Has Isabel said something to them?

There's a kind of complicity among them, the same complicity as between Isabel and my father. She has the gift of being sympathetic, of provoking admiration, confidence.

She is so good, so understanding!

She'd be better advised to take care, because one of these days I might reach my limit. I have set myself a course of conduct and am sticking to it, but I'm beginning to grit my teeth.

I did not drive the girls back to Litchfield, leaving this chore to my wife. On purpose. So that she could cook up her schemes with them at her leisure. I defied her, basically.

'You mustn't pay attention to your father's strange behaviour, children. He's going through a difficult phase . . . Ray's accident really shook him, and his nerves have not recovered yet . . .'

'Why does he drink, Mommy?'

She could tell them that I don't drink more than any of our friends. She definitely doesn't do that.

'Because of his nerves, as I said. To steady himself.'

'Sometimes, he looks at us as if he barely knows us . . .'

'I know. He shuts himself up inside . . . I spoke to Dr Warren about that, and he went to see him.'

'Dad is sick?'

'It's not an illness, properly speaking . . . It's in his mind. He gets these ideas . . .'

'Is it what they call a nervous breakdown?'

'Perhaps . . . It's like that. It happens often, at his age . . .'

Is that how all three of them talk about me? I'd swear to it. I can just hear them. Isabel's soft, indulgent voice as she bestows upon the children the limpidity of her gaze . . .

How reassuring it is to be looked at like that! You feel as if you were diving into a fresh, cool and generous soul that is immune to the passing years.

I'm furious. At the office, my secretary is beginning to watch me uneasily as well. If this continues, everyone will start feeling sorry for me.

Sorry, or afraid?

I can feel Higgins' confusion. For this old rogue, life is simple. It's every man for himself. Anything goes, as long as it's legal. And there are a thousand normal ways of getting around the law.

It's his job. He practises law with a quiet effrontery, without any qualms of conscience.

Lieutenant Olsen passed me at the wheel of his police car when I was on my way to the post office, and he gave me a desultory wave. Does what happened to Ray still bother him? His kind, when they get an idea in their heads . . .

Fine! So what! I telephoned Mona, from the office. Openly. My secretary and even Higgins could hear what I was saying, because except when someone is with a client we usually leave our doors open.

At first, since the phone rang a long time, I was afraid that she hadn't come back from Long Island, where she had gone to spend a few days with friends who have a place out there, with horses and a yacht. I don't know them. She didn't tell me their name, and I didn't ask.

They had many friends, she and Ray. She'd already had lots of them before meeting him. Often, when we were walking in the streets, people would greet her more or less familiarly, some of them calling out:

'Mona, hello!'

Since I am with her, I also wave, clumsily, without asking any questions. Occasionally she'll tell me, as if it explained everything, 'That's Harris . . .' or else, 'That's Helen . . .'

Harris who? Helen who? People known, probably, in the worlds of theatre, film or television. Ray spent much of his time, with the Millers, on budgets for television shows. It had become his specialty and was probably the reason why he asked his wife not to do such work any more, which would have put him in an awkward position.

But now? Won't Mona feel like working again? She hasn't spoken to me about it. Our intimacy belongs to a different domain. There is a whole part of her life that is unknown to me.

'Hello, Mona? . . . It's Donald, yes.'

'How was your vacation?'

'Not good . . . And you? . . . On Long Island?'

'A little crazy . . . I didn't have a moment to myself . . . Every day, more friends would arrive, even ten or twenty at a time . . .'

'Did you go out riding?'

'I even took a tumble, luckily without hurting myself.'

'Any sailing?'

'Twice, I'm all tanned . . .'

'Are you free tomorrow?'

'Wait, what day is it? . . .'

'Wednesday.'

'Eleven o'clock?'

'I'll be at your place at eleven.'

That was our hour, when she was at her toilette, the time I enjoyed the most, with a feeling of abandon, of complete intimacy.

The next day the sky was clear, a lavender-blue, with those golden clouds, over the mountains, that seem to have been put there once and for all, as if in a painting. Only on certain evenings do those clouds disappear or stretch out in long, almost red bands.

I drove along happily.

'You'll be back this evening?'

'Probably . . .'

Does Isabel wonder why I stay overnight in New York less and less frequently? Does she suppose that something has changed between Mona and me?

Or else that I'm beginning to get a grip on myself, to avoid compromising myself any further?

I hate her.

I looked for a parking place for a long time before entering the building on 56th Street. I hurried to the elevator. I rang the doorbell. The door opened immediately, and there was Mona in a lightweight tailored suit of emerald green, as well as a little white hat tilted over her left ear.

I was speechless. She was surprised, as if she hadn't expected to produce such an effect.

'My poor Donald . . .'

I don't like being poor Donald, even for her. I could only take her in my arms when she welcomed me in her peignoir.

'Disappointed?'

Still, we kissed. It's true that her face was tanned, which helps to change her.

'This morning I felt like taking a walk with you in Central Park . . . Do you mind?'

My face cleared. It was a nice idea. The weather was just right. We had not yet celebrated spring together.

'Would you like to drink something before we go?'

'No . . .'

She turned towards the kitchen.

'I won't be back for lunch, Janet . . .'

'Fine, madam . . .'

'If anyone phones for me, I'll be back at around two or three o'clock.'

It wasn't the first time we had strolled along the sidewalks, but the air was lighter than usual, the sunshine quite cheerful, the sky of an astonishing purity behind the skyscrapers.

In front of the Plaza, we saw the scattering of carriages that await tourists and lovers. For one second, I thought about climbing into one of them. Mona was paying no attention. Her hand was resting on my arm, lightly, without insistence.

'How are Mildred and Cecilia?'

'Quite well. They spent their vacation with us. We took several hikes and even went to Cape Cod . . .'

We were heading slowly towards the lake where Ray and I used to skate in the winter when we were students, treating ourselves to a night in New York.

I felt a stronger pressure on my arm from the white-gloved hand.

'I must speak to you, Donald . . .'

It's funny. It wasn't in my back, but in my head that I felt a cold rush and I said, in a voice I hardly recognized:

'Yes?'

'We're old pals, aren't we? You're the best pal I've ever had . . .'

Mothers were watching over children toddling about. A ragged man, who had nothing more to hope for, was sleeping on a bench, so wretched that you had to look away.

We were walking slowly. Head down, I was looking at the gravel passing by under my shoes.

'Do you know John Falk?'

I'd read his name somewhere. He was familiar enough, but at that moment I couldn't place him. I did not try. I awaited the verdict. Because all this was going to end in a verdict, sure as fate.

'He's the producer of the three best series on CBS.'

I had nothing to say. I could hear the noises in the park, the birds, the children's voices, the traffic along Fifth Avenue. I saw ducks smoothing their feathers on the lawn and others swimming, tracing triangular wakes.

'We've known each other for a long time, he and I . . . He's forty . . . He's been divorced for three years and has a little girl . . .'

She added quickly, to get it over with: 'We intend to get married, Donald . . .'

I said nothing. I couldn't have said a thing.

'Are you sad?'

I almost laughed, because of that word. Sad? I was utterly crushed. I was . . . It was beyond explanation. There was nothing left any more, that's all.

Up until then, I had had something left, I had Mona left, even though our liaison wasn't a real one, even though there was no question of love between us.

I saw the boudoir again, the movement of her lips towards the red lipstick, the peignoir she'd let drop down behind her . . .

'Please forgive me . . .'

'For what?'

'For hurting you . . . I can tell I'm hurting you . . .'

'A little,' I said finally, using a ridiculously feeble word myself.

'I should have talked to you about it earlier . . . I've been hesitating for a month now . . . I didn't know what to decide. It even occurred to me to have you meet John and to ask your advice . . .'

We did not look at each other. She had thought of that. That's why she had led me into the park. Walking among others out for a stroll, you're obliged to control yourself.

'When do you plan on . . .'

'Oh! Not right away . . . There are the legal delays to observe . . . We'll also have to find another apartment, because Monique will live with us.'

So, the little girl was named Monique.

'Her father obtained custody of her. He absolutely adores her . . .'

Of course! Of course! And in the meantime, was this John Falk, since that was his name, already sleeping in the big bed at 56th Street?

Probably. Like friends, as Mona says. No: those two, not like friends, since they were going to be married.

'I'm dreadfully sorry, Donald . . . We'll stay good friends, won't we?'

And then what?

'I spoke to John about you.'

'Did you tell him the truth?'

'Why not? He doesn't take me for a virgin . . .'

The word shocked me, spoken aloud, suddenly, in the middle of the sunny park. I am not in love with Mona, I swear it. No one will believe me, and yet it is the truth.

It isn't only 'woman' that she represents to me, it's . . .

It's just everything! And it's nothing! It must be nothing, since she could cut the thread so easily.

She was going to go back to television work. I would see her on my screen, back there in Brentwood, sitting next to Isabel in the library.

'I thought that we might lunch together somewhere, wherever you like . . .'

'Is he the one who'll be calling between two and three?'

'Yes.'

'He knows I'm in town?'

'Yes.'

'He knows you've taken me to Central Park?'

'No . . . I thought of that while getting dressed.'

Not while getting dressed in front of me, with her quiet immodesty. While getting dressed alone. In Janet's company, rather.

'It's going to be difficult, Janet . . .'

'He'll understand, madam.'

'Of course he'll understand, but I'm still going to make him suffer . . .'

'If we had to give up everything that makes others suffer . . .'

Mona lit a cigarette, glancing at me out of the corner of her eye, and I smiled at her. Well, it was meant to be a smile.

'You'll come to see me?'

'I don't know . . .'

That was no. I had nothing in common with Mr and Mrs Falk. Nor with the little girl named Monique.

Girls, I had two of them.

The sun seemed to me to be shining harder than in previous days. We went inside the bar at the Plaza.

'Two double martinis . . .'

I hadn't asked her what she was having. Perhaps, with Falk, she drank something else? For the last time, I observed our tradition.

'Cheers, Donald . . .'

'Cheers, Mona . . .'

That was the hardest part. Saying her name, I almost, stupidly, burst into tears. Those two syllables . . .

What's the point of trying to explain? I saw myself in the mirror, between the bottles.

'Where would you like to have lunch?'

She left the choice to me. It was my day. My last day. So it was important that everything go as well as possible.

'We can go to our little French restaurant . . .'

I shook my head. I preferred a crowd, a place without memories.

We had lunch at the Plaza, and the main room was full. I suggested foie gras, almost derisively, and she agreed. Then lobster. A gala luncheon!

'Would you like crêpes Suzette?'

'Why not?'

She thought to please me by accepting. I knew that she was checking the clock from time to time.

I didn't hold it against her. She had given me what she could give me, kindly, with a warm, animal tenderness, and I was the one left in her debt.

At one point, I saw her hand flat on the tablecloth just as I had seen it on the parquet, that January night, and I felt the same desire to reach for that hand . . .

'Be brave, Donald . . .'

She had guessed.

'If you knew how this hurts me . . .' she sighed.

Then we walked to her place. I wanted to stammer, 'One last time, yes?'

It seemed to me it would be easier, afterwards . . .

I looked up at the windows of the fourth-floor apartment; I entered the lobby.

'Goodbye, Donald . . .'

'Farewell, Mona . . .'

She threw herself into my arms and with no thought of her make-up gave me a very long, very deep kiss.

'I'll never forget,' she panted.

Then, very quickly, feverishly, she opened the elevator door.

## 3.

That was one month ago, and my hatred of Isabel has only grown. As was to be expected, she understood right away, seeing me come home. I wasn't even drunk. I hadn't felt the need to drink.

Driving home along the Taconic Parkway, I was drawing a kind of mental picture of the life awaiting me, from waking to bedtime, with the movements, the comings and goings from one room to another, the post office, my office, my secretary, who would soon be leaving us, lunch, my office, my clients, the mail, the glass of Scotch before dinner, the meal together, the television, a newspaper or a book . . .

I did not omit a single detail. On the contrary, I itemized them carefully, as if in Indian ink.

It was an engraving, an album of engravings, the day of a man named Donald Dodd.

Isabel said nothing, I'd known that in advance. I had also foreseen that she would feel no pity and I would not have wanted any. She did manage, however, to hide her triumph, to keep her eyes impassive.

Then, over the following days, she went back to observing me, the way one observes a patient, wondering if he will die or recover.

I was not dying. My mechanism functioned without a hitch. I had been well trained. My movements remained the same, as did the words I spoke, my behaviour at the table, the office, in my armchair in the evening.

Why was she continuing to spy on me? What was she hoping for?

She wasn't satisfied, I could feel that. She needed something else. My complete annihilation?

I was not annihilated. The following week, Higgins was surprised not to see me go off to New York. My secretary as well.

The week after that, he was relieved, understanding that what he must have called my affair was over.

And so, I was going to re-enter the world of upright, normal people. I had had a kind of moral flu from which I was quite slowly recovering.

Higgins behaved kindly towards me, encouragingly, coming several times a day to my office to speak to me about matters he would once have reported to me with a few words in passing.

Did not my interest in life require rekindling? I met Warren, too, at the post office, where lots of people come to pick up their morning mail. Remembering the reception I'd given him the last time, he hesitated to come over but finally made up his mind.

'You're looking well, Donald . . .'

Of course!

I avoided going to New York, even when it was useful. I tried to arrange everything on the phone and through correspondence. One day, when my presence there was indispensable, I asked Higgins to go instead, and he hastened to accept.

That meant that I was cured, or almost.

If they could have known, every last one of them, how I hated her! But she was the only one who knew.

For I had understood. I had sought the meaning of her look for a long time. I had made various suppositions without thinking of the quite simple truth.

I had detached myself from her. I had broken the circle. I was out of her reach.

For that, she would never forgive me. I was her possession, like the house, the girls, Brentwood and our daily routine.

I had escaped and I was looking at her from outside, I was looking at her with hatred, because she had possessed me for too long, because she had suffocated me, because she had kept me from living.

All right! I had chosen her. I have admitted that and I repeat it. That was not reason enough. But she was still the living image, there, right next to me, in the bed next to mine, of all that I had begun to hate.

I could not take it out on the whole world and its institutions. I could not spit their truths and mine into the faces of millions of human beings.

She was there.

As Mona had been there, for a moment, to do her best representing life.

Isabel knew all that. The qualities attributed to her by others either did exist or they didn't, but there is one that she had to the supreme degree: the ability to rummage through the souls of others, and mine in particular.

She was now doing so to her heart's content, searching all day long, sensing that there was nothing left but a façade and that if this cracked, there would be nothing left.

To see me reduced to nothing! What a marvellous feeling! What matchless revenge.

'It was so good of Isabel . . .'

To live with a man like me, obviously. To put up with what she's had to put up with these past months.

'He didn't bother to hide . . .'

In the evening, I was having more and more trouble getting to sleep and, after an hour lying motionless, I sometimes went into the bathroom to take a sleeping pill.

She knew this. I'm convinced that she avoided falling asleep before I did to enjoy my insomnia, to hear the mysterious rustling of my thoughts.

It wasn't so much Mona's face that haunted me, and I'm not sure if Isabel had guessed that. It was the bench. The red-painted bench. The din of the storm and the door banging in a steady rhythm, the snow that, each time, blew a little farther into the barn.

Ray, with Patricia, in the bathroom. I would have liked to be in his place. I wanted Patricia. One day, when the Ashbridges came back from Florida . . .

Ray was dead. His apartment in Sutton Place that had cost him so much, with its aggressive luxury he had flaunted so ironically, had been dismantled and was now inhabited by a film star.

His wife, Mona, was going to become Mrs Falk. A friend of his. A producer with whom he'd done business.

He had thought about suicide, and death had arrived without him having to lift a finger.

The lucky stiff!

My father kept publishing his *Citizen* and writing articles for two or three dozen elderly readers.

Had Isabel told him that it was over with Mona? Had he been glad like the others, telling himself that I was returning at last to the fold?

I could not bear her eyes any more. I would sometimes look away. I had already stopped brushing her cheek in the morning and evening. She had not mentioned it. I may be wrong, but I think there might have been a glimmer of hope in her eyes.

If I was reacting like that, wasn't it because I'd been affected? Indifferent, I would have continued the routine without noticing anything, without finding it painful.

It was practically a declaration of war. I was becoming her enemy, an enemy who lived in the house, next to her, ate at the same table, slept in the same room.

The month of May had begun gloriously, with days as warm as summertime. I was already wearing my cotton suit, my straw hat.

At the office, the air conditioning was on. Mornings, before I went there, I would dive into the pool and I did the same after coming home in the evening.

Isabel had adopted other hours; not once had she been in the pool at the same time as I was.

'Have you a lot of work?'

'Enough to keep me busy and pay our bills . . .'

The house, which we owned, was worth around sixty thousand dollars. Many years earlier, I had taken out life insurance for one hundred thousand dollars, which had seemed an enormous sum at the time, because I was only just starting out.

Every year, I bought a few stocks.

If I were to go off alone, without saying anything, to melt into the anonymous swarm, neither my wife nor my daughters would find themselves in financial difficulties.

Go where? At night, in my bed, I sometimes thought of the man in Central Park, the one sleeping on a bench at noon, his mouth open, in view of passers-by.

He needed no one. Nor did he need to pretend. He did not worry about people's opinions, good manners, what must be done or not done.

And whenever the police picked him up, he could go back to his snoring.

I wasn't obliged to take such a deep plunge. I could have . . .

But why? I had already escaped, *in situ*, in a way. I had cut the strings. The marionette was still moving, but no one was manipulating it any longer.

Except Isabel. She was there, lying on her back in her bed, silent, listening to my breathing, guessing at my phantoms. She was waiting for the moment when, giving up, I would get up to go and take my two sleeping tablets. These days, I needed two. Soon, I would need three. Was it more serious than drinking?

I had been tempted to drink. Sometimes, when I looked at the liquor cabinet, I wanted to grab the first bottle at hand and drink straight from it, no doubt like the guy in Central Park.

Exactly what was she waiting for? For me to begin screaming with rage? Or pain? Or . . .

I was not screaming, and so she provoked me. When I would get up to take my tablets, she might ask me in a soft voice, as if speaking to a child or a sick person:

'You're not sleeping, Donald?'

She could see that I wasn't sleeping, right? I wasn't a sleepwalker. So, why ask me that question?

'Maybe you should go and see Warren . . .'

Oh sure! Sure! She was trying to convince me that I was ill. She must have been convincing others, too.

'He's going through a difficult period, I don't know why . . . Dr Warren doesn't understand at all . . . He believes that it's a mental problem . . .'

The guy who has a mental illness . . .

I could get the picture perfectly, in people's minds, the sympathetic faces. I had already been the guy who had a mistress and might soon get divorced. Now I was the husband who is getting weird.

'Just yesterday, I passed him in the street, and he didn't recognize me . . .'

As if I tried to recognize the faceless people who go by!

She was depraved. I'm not the one who is busy drawing up a dossier. She is. Patiently, in minute detail, the way you weave a tapestry. She does sometimes do exactly that. Two of the living room chairs are upholstered in her handiwork.

She weaves . . . She weaves . . .

And she watches me ferociously while waiting for me to crack up.

Isn't she afraid?

# 4.

I am calm, with a lucidity that I believe few men have attained. This is not a speech for the defence. I am not looking to exonerate myself. I am not writing this for anyone in particular.

It is three o'clock in the morning. Today is 27 May, and the day was stiflingly hot. Nothing out of the ordinary happened. I had a lot of work at the office and I completed it conscientiously. By the way, I now know that my secretary is pregnant; after a few months' leave, however, she intends to come back to work.

That is no longer of any importance to me, but it will be to Higgins.

Last night, as soon as I went to bed, my sheets became damp, because we don't have air conditioning. The complicated arrangement of the rooms in the house makes it almost impossible to install.

At half past midnight I was not asleep and went to take my two tablets. She did not speak to me but she followed me with her wide-open eyes. She literally caught me right when I got out of bed, watched me head for the bathroom and, when I came out, there were her eyes, waiting to lead me back to bed.

Sleep did not come. The tablets have lost their power. I don't dare increase the dose without Warren's advice, and I'm not eager to see Warren at the moment.

She is lying on her back. So am I. My eyes are open, because it's even worse when I close them and I can hear my heart beat.

I could, if I listened hard, hear hers.

Two hours have passed. It's unbelievable how many images can scroll through a brain in two hours. The one I saw most again was the hand, on the living room floor.

I wonder why that hand has taken on such importance. I have held the entire body in my arms. I know it in its most minute details, in all kinds of light.

No! It's the hand that comes back to me, on the floor, near my mattress. I turned on the bedside lamp, got up and went to the bathroom.

'Don't you feel well, Donald?'

Because I don't usually get up twice.

I swallowed another tablet, then one more, to have done with this insomnia.

When I went back into the bedroom, she was sitting on her bed and looking at me.

Hadn't she almost reached her goal? Hadn't she just heard the first crack?

I did not think anything over. The action was spontaneous, and I performed it calmly. Opening the night table drawer, I grabbed the revolver.

She was still looking at me, without frowning. She was still defying me.

Wasn't my first thought to point the gun at myself, as Ray had been tempted to do?

Probably. I wouldn't dare swear to it.

She looked at the short barrel, then at my face. What I am sure of is this: a smile flickered over her face, and there was, in her blue eyes, a gleam of triumph.

I shot at the chest and felt no emotion. The eyes were still staring at me, motionless, so then I fired two more shots.

In those eyes.

I will telephone Lieutenant Olsen to tell him what has happened. People will talk about a crime of passion, and there will certainly be questions about Mona, who has nothing to do with it.

They'll have me examined by a psychiatrist.

What difference will it make to me to be in prison, since I have been there all my life?

I've just called Olsen. He did not seem too surprised. He said, 'I'm coming right away . . .'

And he added:

'Above all, don't do anything foolish . . .'